WHATEVER HAPPENED TO SOFIE LE SAUX?

DAVID B. LYONS

ISBN: 978-1-7398552-5-3

Created with Vellum

FACT

600,000 people are reported missing throughout Europe every year. Half of which are children.

That means, more specifically, that 5,700 children go missing throughout the continent every single week.

Or..

815 children

every

single

day.

LENNY

11:30

Lenny's never felt comfortable with heights. Which is why the calm usually offered by the floor-to-ceiling windows as he paces the carpeted corridor of the fifty-second floor of The Empire Building has been failing to attract his glance.

When he stops at the glass elevator shaft, he allows a cringe to trickle its way through his jaws, before stabbing a finger against the flashing digital arrow pointing downwards. He squints to soak in his reflection in the glass while the elevator rises with a distant whizz, noticing he is wringing his hands. Again. With a huff, he shoves his hands into the deep pockets of his yellow puffer jacket, then spins on the spot to find himself staring down at the maze of rust-orange rooftops five hundred feet below...

And from not being able to glance at the view as he walked, he finds himself enamoured by it; engrossed particularly by the sight of the St. Vitus cathedral, standing proud amongst the web of rust-orange roofed homes. His fixation erodes the cringing... but only momentarily.

The cringing began as soon as he had strode out of the penthouse office of Prague's tallest building, the silence he left in that room screaming at him.

He squints through the rust-orange roof tiled houses, towards the grey roofed tiled houses of the suburbs in the distance, noting how jam-packed every street of Prague truly is. When the elevator arrives with a swoosh behind him, Lenny kisses his lips at the dramatic view, then swiftly swivels his slight frame inside the glass box. And when he pushes at the button marked 'zero' he feels a self-punch to the gut, reigniting the cringing. Taking him down as swiftly as the elevator.

'I'm a fucking eejit,' he whispers to himself as he descends in the glass box. 'A fucking eejit.'

He replays his answers over and over again in his head, wincing at every hesitation and stutter he can hear. Until that's all he can hear.

To distract from his own embarrassment, he slips his phone out of the pocket of the yellow puffer jacket he wore over his brand-new navy suit and holds his thumb above the screen... waiting... and waiting...

When the glass box finally reaches ground zero, and the doors slide open with a swish, Lenny steps into the marble lobby and immediately stabs his thumb to the screen, before lifting the phone to his ear.

'Hul-ho.' She answers before one ring tone has completed; her accent thick. 'How d'it go, Len-ny?'

'Ugh,' he scoffs, scratching the stubble above his ear. 'I mean, I made a fuckin' ass of myself, didn't I, Celina? I was stuttering like a prick... and blinking. Blinking all the time. And my hands kept wringing under the desk. But it was a glass desk, so they could see my hands. I mean...'

'Oh, Len-ny, I bet you did great. You're just being hard on yourself.'

'Uuugh, I dunno,' he says, his voice dejected. 'It's just, y'know, when they ask questions and stuff, I'm just not that quick at answering them, am I? I need time to think things through. I've never been good like that.'

'I bet you did great, Len-ny,' Celina says. 'Why are you always being hard on yourself?'

'How are the boys?' he asks, chicaning the conversation.

'They're great, Len-ny. Of course they are. They've been smiling every day since you moved here. They're smiling now. I will send a photo...'

'So, they're not missing me?'

'No,' Celina says, pushing it out with a giggle. 'I bet you miss them more.'

Lenny stops pacing, his pointed leather shoes screeching against the stain-marble tiles of The Empire Tower's extravagant lobby.

'I miss them so much,' he says. 'Is that weird, Celina? It's been, like, what twenty hours? How can I miss them so much?'

'It's not weird, Len-ny,' she replies. 'It's the first day you've been away from them since... since Sally died. Yes, Len-ny. I can tell they miss you. But they will be so happy when you get home tonight. They're out in the garden smiling, Len-ny. They're smiling. That's all we can ever ask of them. That's all we can ever ask of anyone.' Lenny holds his eyes closed, already feeling the warmth embrace of the hugs he will engulf his boys in when he arrives home. 'But it is not important how we are feeling here,' Celina follows up with. 'It is only important how you are feeling right now, Len-ny.'

'Ugh,' he says, shaking his head. He begins pacing again towards the grand entrance he had walked through an hour previous, his chest thumping with anticipation. 'I'm grand. A little knackered. I didn't really sleep last night, y'know? The hotel bed was just... different. And I just kept thinking of the interview. Over and over again.'

'What questions did they ask you?' Celina asks.

'Ahh, mostly about my experience. They asked about the Betsy Taylor case a lot.'

'And?'

'I dunno. I'm confused about that case. Always have been. Everyone seems to think I solved it, don't they? I didn't really. But I'll take it... I guess it got me in here in the first place, didn't it?' He stares around the grand marble lobby as he continues to stride across it, the sheen of wealth flickering and blinking back at him. 'I'm just... I'm cringing that I stuttered and hesitated so much. And I was blinking. I barely stopped blinking, Celina. And my hands... Jesus.'

He slaps a palm to the top of his bald, pale head.

'I bet they loved you, Len-ny.'

'Oh, I dunno about that,' he says. 'I think I felt a bit intimidated, y'know. It was three grey-haired blokes sitting across a long glass table staring at me, asking me question after question, judging my answer after answer. They were judging me with their eyebrows, Celina.'

'Eyebrows? What are you talking about, Len-ny?' she says with her familiar giggle.

'The main one, in the middle, he had like a thick head of white hair and jet-black eyebrows that pointed downwards. Like upside down hairy Nike logos. He's the chief exec of the PTU. Dr. Chuck Vol—'

A finger on Lenny's shoulder causes him to snap his lips shut, and as he takes the phone from his ear, he swivels on the spot... slowly. Taking in, firstly, the thick mop of white hair in front of him, then the jet-black eyebrows pointing downwards like two hairy Nike logos.

'Uh, Celina,' Lenny says. 'I, uh... I gotta go.'

He stabs his thumb against the red button on the screen, then gulps. As silently as he can.

'Sorry to disturb your call,' Eyebrows says, a sheet of paper slapped against his silver tie.

'That's...uh, okay,' Lenny says, his eyes blinking rapidly.

'Moon,' Eyebrows says. 'Welcome to the PTU.'

'Huh?' Lenny says, his nose squishing. 'Are you... are you serious? I thought I sounded like a stuttering wreck in that interview—'

'Look,' Eyebrows says. 'You're a terrible interviewee, Moon. But we believe you to be a fine investigator. Besides,' he says, stepping closer to Lenny and lowering his baritone. 'We are shit short of investigators given the amount of missing people, so you could have shat on the glass table in that interview, and we'd still have hired you.'

Lenny shakes his head.

'O-kay,' he says slowly, unsure. He's been unsure of Dr Chuck Volgt from the moment he sat in front of him a little less than an hour ago, glaring at his unique eyebrows. 'It would be an honour to be part of the PTU team.'

Lenny holds his hand out. But Dr Volgt doesn't notice, or pretends not to notice. So, Lenny tucks his hand back into the pocket of his yellow puffer jacket, remembering as he does so that he never took the puffer jacket off for the interview, like Celina had insisted. What was the point in paying two-hundred and twenty euros for a brand-new navy suit when he never got to show it off. He was only bringing the yellow puffer jacket for good luck. But he was supposed to leave it outside the interview room. Not walk in enveloped by it.

'You'll find the People Trafficking Unit a professionally-run organisation,' Dr Volgt says. 'But it's professionally run because its investigators don't ask questions. Not in here.' The beady eyes beneath the bushy eyebrows flicker a little. 'You guys ask questions out there.' He points towards the grand entrance. 'Not in here.'

'Sure,' Lenny says, a smile itching on the corners of his lips, his head beginning to nod enthusiastically. 'When do I, uh... when do I start?'

Dr Volgt slaps the sheet of paper he had been clutching to his chest against Lenny's oversized jacket.

'You start right now.'

'Right now?' Lenny asks, his voice high-pitched as he peels the sheet away from his jacket to stare down at an image of a young girl smiling back at him.

'We believe she was swiped this morning. Will need finding by tonight... Otherwise she's gone, Moon. Gone for good. Sofie Le Saux will be traded before you and I are taking our first bite of croissants in the morning...'

SOFIE

I am bored. Prague is boring. Much more boring than Paris. In Paris I had friends. A friend. But here, I don't have any friends. Not one. I would love to go back to Paris. Even though the orphanage in Paris is not as clean or as nice as the one in Prague. But at least I could talk to people, even if they didn't talk back. I could speak French or English in Paris. Everyone in the orphanage there spoke French or English. Nobody speaks French or English here. Nobody really speaks at all. Not to me.

They are trying to teach me some Czech language at the new orphanage. But it is too hard. And too boring. So, so boring. Everything in Prague is boring. Everything at the orphanage is boring. And that is why I take a long, long walk away from the orphanage in the mornings after I wake up. To get away from everybody. And everything. I just walk and walk and walk and walk through the fields, until I get hungry. Then I walk all the way back to the orphanage and eat what all of the other children didn't eat for breakfast. The food at the orphanage is not nice. And it can be smelly. So, so smelly. But it is still nicer than the grey soup I used to eat almost every day in the Paris orphanage. In Paris I had a friend, but grey soup. In Prague, I have no friends. But the lunches are different every day. Even if the food is really smelly.

I was supposed to have a family by now. I was told by the nuns in my Paris orphanage that I was going to be adopted. That a man and woman in the Czech Republic wanted to be my father and mother. That's why I was moved to the orphanage in Prague, ready to be taken home by my new family. Only my new family never came. I heard two of the adults at the orphanage talking about me a few weeks ago. They said that the family who were supposed to adopt me, adopted another girl instead. A younger girl. Who was just five years old. From Greece. They weren't coming to adopt me. Nobody was coming to adopt me. And I was just going to stay in the Prague orphanage. With no family. And no friends.

That's why I just walk and walk and walk and walk all morning long. I just throw my bag on my back with my Kindle and my bottle filled with water inside it. I bring my Kindle with me everywhere I go. For two reasons. Because I love to read. And because it reminds me of Anais-Marie. Anais-Marie was my friend in the Paris orphanage. My best friend in the whole wide world. Until the day I first got my Kindle. The exact same day.

I like to walk through these fields because they're so quiet. And green. And sometimes yellow. I never see people in the fields. That's why I love walking around here. Sometimes I think I should go into Prague city and beg for money. And if I get some I wouldn't have to eat the breakfast leftovers when I got back to the orphanage. But the two times I tried to beg in Prague, everybody walked by me without looking up. So, I just walk the fields instead. In the quiet. I think I will like quiet for all of my life. I read in my notes one day back in the Paris orphanage that I was a quiet baby. That I never cried. Or screamed. I also read in the same notes that my real father left my real mother before I was born. The notes said he didn't want anything to do with her, or her baby. That made me sad. For me. And for my mother. Until I read down the page and it said she didn't want me either when I was born. She left me in the orphanage in Paris instead. She probably thought I would find a new father and mother. But I haven't. The closest I ever came to having a father and a mother was a few months ago when I was told a man and a woman from the Czech Republic wanted me as their daughter. I was so happy. So, so happy. But that father and mother did the same as my real father and mother. They left me in the orphanage. They didn't want me either.

I've only passed two women on this walk so far this morning. One of them looked at me and said, 'ahoj'. I smiled and said, 'ahoj' back. I wanted to stop, and ask her if she had any money, or if she had any food. But I didn't. Because she walked past too fast. It's more difficult to get food or money from people in Prague. In Paris, I knew the words. I knew the people better. But here, nobody knows French. And nobody knows English. They didn't read all the books I've read. Or watched all the films I've watched. My favourite films are in English. Me and Anais-Marie used to watch all of the Disney movies on the TV at the Paris orphanage together. My favourite movies are *Toy Story 2*. And *Toy Story 4*. My favourite book is probably *The Twits*. By Roald Dahl. Or any *Bunny versus Monkey*. I love those books, too. But *The Twits* has been my favourite since before I had my Kindle. So I always say that's my favourite. Even though nobody ever asks me what my favourite book is. I prefer to read than watch movies. Now that I don't have a friend to watch movies with. *The Twits* and *Toy Story* are funny. And silly. I think that's why I like them. I like funny and silly things. I think I would be a funny and silly person if I wasn't sad. I think I was silly and funny with Anais-Marie when we used to be friends. She was funny and silly. And that made me funny and silly. My favourite joke is: 'What is the loudest dessert?' — 'I-Screeeaaam!!' I would scream really loud when I told that joke. Only I don't tell it anymore. Not out loud. I only tell it to myself inside my head when I want to try to feel happy. I did tell it to one of the adults at the Prague orphanage when I first moved in. But she didn't laugh. She just looked annoyed that I was screaming. So I don't ever say that joke no more.

'Anjou holcicko,' a voice says. A man's voice.

It makes me scared a little. Because I don't usually see people when I am walking through the fields. I look up and see a man staring down at me. He might be homeless, too. His beard is all dirty and grey. And he looks tired. As if he didn't go to sleep. I wouldn't probably get any money from him.

I shrug my shoulders. Because I don't know what he is saying. I know 'Ahoj' is hello. But I don't know the other word he said. It sounded funny.

'You, uh.. speak English?' he asks.

'Yes!' I say, nodding. 'I speak English.'

I smile at him. And he smiles at me. A friendly smile.

'Good,' he says. 'Would you like a mint?'

He holds a silver wrapper out.

'Yes, please,' I say, nodding. I always say 'please'. Or 's'il vous plait'. It's nice to be polite. I read that in a book called *The Lion In Me*. Polite people are the nicest people. And it's easy to be polite. Which means it's easy to be nice. You just have to smile. And say 'please'. Or 's'il vous plait.'

He pinches at the wrapper and a white mint pops out at me. So, I look back up at his hairy face, then back down at the mint, before grabbing it. And popping it into my mouth.

'It's nice,' I say, swirling it across my tongue.

'You hungry?' he asks.

'I'm really hungry,' I say, nodding.

'Okay,' he says. 'Follow me...'

LENNY

11:55

Lenny races his shadow through the maze of streets lined by rust-orange roof tiles — the sheet clutched to his chest — until he comes to a sudden, panting stop, the soles of his pointed shoes skidding against the chalked pavement. He stares down the flight of narrow concrete steps, in front of him, then grips the orange rail and shuffles himself towards the dark hole beneath... until he hears a shricking, hissing, piercing screech, and the lights turn on.

'Excuse-y me,' he says, when he reaches the bottom of the concrete steps, barking his awful European accent towards a middle-aged woman wearing thick glasses, 'is-a this-a tram going to...' He points at the sheet in his hand, 'Kobylisy?'

'Eno,' the woman responds, nodding. Lenny wasn't confused that her answer sounded like an English 'no' while she was nodding. He knew 'eno' meant 'yes'. It was one of the very few basic words he had learnt on his flight into Prague yesterday afternoon.

'Great,' he says, 'Thanks a mill.'

'Have you got ticket?' the middle-aged woman asks, re-fixing her oversized glasses on the bridge of her nose.

Lenny blinks back at her, scratching at the stubble over his ear.

'Eh...' he mumbles, looking around himself.

'That way,' she says, pointing towards three bright-yellow tin boxes along the back wall of the platform. Brighter yellow than Lenny's jacket.

He glances over his shoulder at them, then back at the woman—squinting at how large her eyes looked behind her bottle-thick lenses.

'How do I, uh?' he asks, shrugging. But the woman spins on the spot, to step onto the tram that had screeched to a stop just as Lenny was descending into the underground. She has no more time for the tourist's questions.

He swivels his pointed shoes, then shuffles towards the yellow boxes, his breathing sharp and swift as he attempts to catch up with himself. He pushes a finger to the screen, then squints at the Czech instructions in front of him, huffing, just as a bell chimes behind him.

'No-No-Noo,' he shouts, looking back over his shoulder as the doors of the tram slide to a close. He sprints, skidding the soles of his shoes across the tiles of the platform, until his narrow body catches between the doors. He feels a pinch to the groin until the doors hiss again, and begin to slide back open, leaving him to step into a sea of frustrated faces. A familiar self-punch to the gut hits him, and a cringe itches through his jaws, causing him to blink rapidly. He whispers a 'sorry' to nobody in particular, then grips a bright red steel bar tight as the doors re-close.

When the tram pulls off with a hiss, he squints away from the faces staring at him; aware he is yet another tourist catching a free ride on their respected transport system. To distract from the cringing, he stares up at the Czech names on the lined map above the doors that almost cut him in half; his eyes following the lines of the stations north—the direction in which Dr Volgt had told him to ride the tram... Towards Kobylisy—the small suburb on the northern outskirts of Prague where he will find a street called Ladza Street among the maze of terraced grey-bricked houses with even greyer roof-tiles. The street in which Ruthgar Bilic lives.

Dr Volgt had revealed a lot to Lenny upon offering him the job; not just the address of the prime suspect in the Sofie Le Saux case. As Volgt leaned his heavy frame against a marble wall in the lobby of Prague's tallest building, he explained what Lenny's role would entail as a PI within the People Trafficking Unit. The PTU had been founded in 1992 as a branch webbing away from the European Union to help multiply the number of investigators working on the ever-growing missing persons cases throughout the continent. The PTU's data suggest that ninety-four per cent of successful missing children cases, are successful within the first twenty-four hours. After that, missing children can be like ghosts in Europe.

'Your job, Moon,' Dr Volgt told him, 'is to find these kids within day one. As soon as they are reported missing, we want investigators like you to act. Follow the trail while it is hot, then find the kid before they're auctioned.' Dr Volgt fingered Sofie Le Saux's pretty face on the sheet Lenny was gripping. 'There's not much to go on,' the doctor continued. 'Everything we know, you now know. Because everything we know is on that page. Sofie Le Saux was reported missing three hours ago, by another child who lives in the same orphanage as her. The other child watched Sofie walk off into acres of farmland on the outskirts of Kobylisy this morning. Either Sofie disappeared out of thin air. Or she was swiped. By coincidence a known trafficker released from prison two days ago happens to live within twenty-two minutes of where Sofie was last seen. His name is Ruthgar Bilic. He's your lead. As well as the sole reason we sanctioned this as a possible people trafficking case. Take a Metro to Kobylisy...' Lenny scribbled a note on the top of the front page, above Sofie's blonde hair. 'He lives in 22 Ladza Street. It's not a lot to go on. But it's your start, Moon. Look, there are hundreds of cases like this every day throughout Europe. Police forces aren't interested until missing persons are twenty-four hours missing. Which is one hell of a flaw in the system. That flaw becomes even more alarming when we know that the first twenty-four hours are the most crucial in any missing person's case. That's where we come in. The PTU. The board of the PTU will sanction an investigation if we feel there's reason to believe the case to be trafficking. Listen,' Dr Volgt leaned in, narrowing his hairy upside Nike-swoosh eyebrows, 'there are two things you should know about being a PI in the PTU, Moon. One, don't expect to solve too many cases. There is no such fucking thing as James Bond in the real Europe. And two, don't get attached. Investigators who get attached to their subjects don't make it past the first three months in this job. That's why we got to keep hiring people like you. Your goal each time is difficult, Moon, but it's also very simple: find the subject within the first twenty-four hours. That lightens the weight from the top of the unit.'

'I...I,' Lenny stuttered, his head nodding. 'I'll do my best.'

'Take a left out of here, then your second right,' Dr Volgt instructed him. 'At the end of that street you'll see an orange M on a signpost. That's the nearest underground line. You'll need to take a Metro to this place,' he said, pointing at the note Lenny had scribbled on top of Sofie's smiling portrait.

Then, without hesitating any more, Lenny raced himself through the maze of white houses topped by rust-orange roof tiles. Turning left. Then spinning around the second right, puffing and panting. Until he suddenly noticed an orange M on a signpost above a dark squared hole.

Lenny stares around the cramped tram, the weight of paranoia lifting from him as he notices the blurred faces around him have turned their attentions away from his bald head, staring blankly at their phones instead. He looks up the tram, then down the tram, realising he may have a better chance of finding Sofie Le Saux than a seat. So, he leans his head back a little, holding the sheet out in front of him, and stares at the portrait again... before flicking the page over.

Name: *Sofie Le Saux*

Age: *7*

Home address: *122 Milkova Orphanage.*

Height: *4'0" approx.*

Appearance: *As front page.*

Background*: Originally French, near Marseilles. Orphaned to a Paris nunnery until she was six years old. Proposed to a family based in Prague for adoption and held in a Prague orphanage while she awaited that family... only for the adoption to fall through. She has remained in that Prague orphanage for the past four months.*

Languages: *Speaks French and English well.*

Wearing: *Blue overalls over white T shirt. Dirty trainers. Hair had a light-blue scrunchie tied into it. Was carrying denim back-pack that had a Kindle, a book. And a pencil case.*

Why PTU chose to investigate: *Police insisting on obligatory twenty-four hours before declaring this a missing person's case. Fellow orphan is adamant Sofie was swiped. There's an off-chance, though it is throwing darts in the dark, that a local man named Ruthgar Bilic could be involved. He had just been released from prison two days ago for a smuggling charge. Possible coincidence, but worth having one of the low-level PIs to look into it. We've marked this as a level 1 PTU operation pretty much based on the coincidence that Bilic was recently released and is a twenty-two-minute drive away. Maybe pass this one to one of the new suckers we recruit today?*

. . .

Lenny puffs out a smile, causing the woman with the thick glasses he had spoken to earlier to glare up into his pale face. Again.

He glances back down, flipping the page over, to stare at Sofie's soft features, noting she's not unlike Betsy Blake. Lenny has solved fifty-seven missing persons cases over the years. But none were quite like the Betsy case. Most were just runaways Lenny managed to track down. The nearest he came to a kidnapping after Betsy was when a father took his kids away from their mother and drove them to a B&B in Donegal. The majority of cases Lenny dealt with were domestic cases. To do with domestic matters. There was never another Betsy Blake. Not until now... Not until he accepted a job with the PTU just half an hour ago.

He squints through Sofie's soft features, past the hint of a smile on the corner of her lips, past her buttoned nose splashed by a dance of freckles, before his head jerks upwards. And he sucks in a sharp breath.

'A Kindle!' he shouts, causing the faces around him to stare back up into his pale face. 'She has her fucking Kindle with her!'

SOFIE

The grass is so tall. I have never walked this far into the fields. Some of it is taller than me. And it's orange. Like a faded orange. It's not green. Or yellow. Not out this far.

'Where we going?' I shout towards him.

'Shhhh,' he says, turning around. 'Nearly there.' He waves his hand at me. He wants me to move faster.

'Good,' I say, jogging towards him.

The mint he gave me is burning my tongue. But I'd eat another hundred of them. A thousand of them. I'm hungry. So, so hungry. But I'm always hungry. So it is not new.

I fix the strap of my bag on my shoulder. Because it's heavier on one side sometimes. It's not the book or the Kindle that is heavy. It's my bottle of water. My bag's always heavier at the start of the day. I stop and drop the bag from one shoulder and unzip it, then take out the bottle. And as I suck from it, I stare back, back through the long grass. I have probably come too far. Even for food.

'Just across this next field,' he whispers over his shoulder. 'Come on!'

He sounds strange. Whispering. Even though we're in the

middle of so many fields and nobody can hear him. Nobody could hear him if he shouted.

We walk some more. Him walking, me trying to jog to keep up with him.... Until he gets down low and shuffles through a bush. When I stare through the bush, I see him reach his hand through, holding his hand out for me. So, I put my hand inside his and he helps pull me through.

'That is my car over here,' he says when I stand back up on the other side, brushing my overalls down.

'Car?' I say.

'Yes,' he says. 'I have food in the car.'

'Oh,' I say. 'Dekuji.'

Dekuji is one of the few words I know in Czech. I learned how to say 'hello', 'please', and 'thank you.' 'Ahoj', 'prism', and 'dekuji'. Because they are the most important words.

When we reach his car he opens the back door, he turns around and grabs my face. Hard. Squeezing it. Squeezing it so hard I want to cry. And scream. But I can't. Because he is squeezing my mouth so hard. He pushes my head onto the back seat of the car and shoves me inside. I try to scream. But he squeezes my mouth, and stares then at me. His face really close up. He looks angry. His eyes are really wide. And he smells. He smells bad.

'Be quiet,' he whispers.

I start breathing really hard the same way he is breathing hard. And he stretches his other arm into the front seat and then brings a roll of black Sellotape to his mouth. When he takes his hand off my mouth to help bite at the Sellotape, I don't try to scream. Because he will hurt me. I think he will hurt me because his eyes are really wide. And scary. So, so scary.

'This will keep you quiet,' he says.

He slaps the Sellotape over my mouth, and I feel as if I can't breathe already. As if I'm going to stop breathing. And die.

He doesn't care that I can't breathe. He steps out of the back of the car and slams the door closed. Loud. So loud I can still hear it in my ears. Then he gets into the front seat. And my breathing gets harder. And faster.

I try to say something to him. But I can only hear 'hmm-mmm, hmmmmmm' inside my own ears.

'Keep your head down, or I will hurt you,' he says, turning around.

So I do. I keep my head down while I try to breathe in through my nose. But I don't like breathing in through my nose. It's hard to breathe in through your nose.

He starts the car and begins driving and as he is driving my hands get sweaty and I wish I said 'no' when he asked me if I want a mint. Then I could have just kept walking through the fields on my own, and I wouldn't be lying in the back of a car with black Sellotape across my mouth. I close my eyes. And when I close my eyes, I feel tears in them. I haven't cried in so long. Even though I probably should cry every day. And every night. Because I have nobody. No friends. No family. I should be sad all the time. But I don't cry. I haven't cried properly since the day I first got my Kindle.

But I'm crying properly now. A tear falls down my cheek. And onto the black Sellotape. So I close my eyes even harder. Because I don't want any more tears to come out. But more do. From both eyes. I try to breathe in much longer through my nose. To try and make my breathing feel right. I can smell petrol. I like the smell of petrol. Sometimes. But right now, I hate it. I hate everything. I even hate myself. I should not have walked so far from the orphanage. I should not have said 'yes' when he asked me if I wanted a mint.

I slide around in the back seat when he turns a corner, and I try to count how many corners we will turn. Two, I think.... Three now, as I slide around the back seat again.Back over to the other side of the car.

I hear children playing. Lots of children. Like a school playground. A school playground with lots and lots of children. Having fun. Playing games. But the children disappear as he drives on..

Turn six... turn seven.... I slide back to the other side of the car.

I want to ask him where he's taking me. But I can't. I can't speak. Not with this black Sellotape across my mouth. So, I just concentrate on my breathing. Through my nose. Out my nose. My eyes still closed.

Turn nine... I think. I think that's nine turns now...

I wipe at the tears from my cheek with my sleeve, then I lift myself up from the backseat and open my eyes, so I can try to stare out the window. The houses are grey around here. Not white. Not bright white like they are around the orphanage. I am so far away. So, so far away. With thick, black Sellotape across my mouth...

When the car slows down I drop to my belly. And then... it stops. Fully stops. The keys turned in the car. The motor stopping. I don't see him, but I hear him. Turning around to me.

'Keep quiet. If you make any noise, I will hurt you.'

I nod my head. And the same sound comes out of my mouth like it did earlier. 'Hmmmmm.'

I hold my eyes closed again. And another tear falls to the black Sellotape just as he gets out of the car. I want to lean back up and look out the window. But I don't. Because I just want to stay quiet. And keep my head down. Like he told me to. So that he doesn't hurt me. I don't want him to hurt me. I just want to go back to the orphanage. So I can eat some leftover breakfast.

The back door opens, and I feel scared. So, so scared. But I still don't look up, or make any noise... I just lie there. My bag pressed into my back. My face down.

Then I feel him. On top of me. And I smell him again. He smells like a bin smells.

'Keep quiet, or I will hurt you,' he whispers into my ear.

I nod my head, and as I do a squeak comes out of my mouth. And I cry. Again. The tears coming even faster this time. Rolling down my cheeks one after the other.

He grabs around my waist, then lifts me out of the car, pulling me over his shoulder. All I can see is the pavement. Then at one grey concrete step with weeds growing out of it. And then into a house. A really smelly house.

LENNY

12:25

Lenny rests a shoulder to the brick wall atop the concrete steps of Kobylisy Metro station and stares through the gaps of the rust-orange rooftops across the street, his phone pressed to his chest, hold music chiming through it.

With the other hand, he is gripping the sheet, re-reading the notes as if he hadn't read them a hundred times on the tram. It came to him the very first time he had read the notes, like a bolt of lightning striking through his ears as he was gripping the bright red bar on the tram. A Kindle! Sofie Le Saux had a Kindle in her backpack when she went missing. Betsy Taylor almost escaped using a Kindle, Lenny instantly remembered. She wrote about it in *Betsy's Basement.* The closest she ever came to getting out of that basement was through the Kindle Gordon Blake had bought for her.

When the hold music cuts, Lenny leans off the wall, and stands to attention.

'Putting you through now, Sir,' a soft voice says. Olette's voice. He recalled her from this morning.

'What is it, Moon?' a gruff voice immediately cuts in.

'Uh, sorry for calling you so soon into starting my new job, Sir, it's just, uh...'

'Get to it, Moon.'

'Sorry, Dr Volgt, it's just... something I noticed in the Sofie Le Saux notes.'

'There's nothing in the Sofie Le Saux notes, Moon. We know nothing about this case. Except that lead we gave you.'

'Sir, look, it says in the notes that Sofie had a Kindle with her when she went missing... I think if we can infiltrate Amazon—'

'Oh, fuck off, Moon,' Volgt spits, snarling his irritation. 'What did I tell you when I offered you the job? I gave you two pieces of advice, did I not? What were they?'

'Uh,' Lenny says, scratching at the stubble behind his ear, 'don't get too attached to any subject, you said.'

'Yes. Don't get too attached to any of your subjects. That was one. And the other...'

Lenny sighs, a deflated puff huffing through him.

'There are no James Bonds.'

'There are no James Bonds,' Volgt repeats. 'Exactly.'

Lenny lets his shoulder fall back on to the brick wall as a dead tone sobs through his phone, beeping the embarrassment up into his face. He stabs a finger to the screen, ending his torture, then tucks his belly in before sucking a cold breath through the gaps in his teeth.

He suffers the familiar impact of a self punch to the gut, like the ones he used to feel when he would cuss and shout at his innocent twin boys.

'What the fuck am I doing?' he says, clutching his stomach.

He slides his back down the brick wall, until his bony ass reaches the dusty concrete. And he sits, staring across the street at the rows of white terraced houses topped with rust-orange rooftops, his eyes lightly blinking.

He'd only flown to Prague for an interview. Not to start a job. When he was staring down from the fifty-second floor of The Empire Tower this morning at the maze of streets below, he could have no idea he was about to get lost among them.

He holds the sheet out again, turning it over and re-reading the one-page of notes, the word 'Kindle' screaming at him, an imaginary clock tick-tocking through his mind. He knew what being a new recruit in the PTU meant. The recruitment process was clear. Then re-emphasised during the interview this morning. Multiple times. They wanted investigators with as much experience as possible. Ex-cops through the continent. Ex-detectives. PI's. Lenny's experience was key to him getting in the door for an interview. The fact that his interviewed flailed was insignificant at that stage. They need guys like him. Quick-minded detectives. Only he never could have thought he'd have to be *this* quick. Twenty-four hours quick. Finding missing persons before the police can legally get involved. No wonder Volgt had told Lenny earlier that he shouldn't expect to find all of his targets. That he shouldn't get attached to his subjects. But fuck the James Bond quip. Investigators are supposed to think outside the box. They're supposed to investigate. It's in the fucking job title...

He drops the sheet to the concrete and pushes himself back to a standing position. Then he clutches his phone and begins to tap a pointed finger against it. When he brings the phone to his ear, a foreign tone is piercing through it.

'Hul-ho,' she says.

'Celina,' he says.

'Len-ny,' she says. 'What is going on?'

'Uh,' he says, pausing, hesitating. 'They, uh... they offered me the job.'

'Yesss!' Celina screams into his ear. 'I knew it! I knew you would do it! When do you start, Len-ny?'

'That's, uh... that's the thing,' Lenny says, staring down at his pointed leather shoes. 'I've already started...'

'Huh?'

'I've already started. I'm on a case right now. A missing girl. Here in Prague. They want me to find her. They need me to find her within twenty-four hours.'

'Twenty-four.. what? Wait. Does this mean you won't be home tonight, Len-ny?'

Lenny looks up and down the street, his eyes now blinking.

'I guess so,' he says. 'I uh... I need you to do something for me,' he continues. 'I need you to find the copy of *Betsy's Basement* I have... somewhere... somewhere in the bedroom, I think. It's important to my investigation. Betsy wrote a chapter in that book about contacting somebody on her Kindle when she was in the basement. I need to find out how she did that...'

'Oh, Len-ny,' Celina says. 'Are you sure you brought that book with you when you moved? I haven't seen it.'

'Yeah... I definitely packed it. Course I did. Betsy signed it for me.'

'Oh-kay,' Celina says. 'Let me go have a look in your bedroom.'

Lenny squints above the rust-orange roof tops as he listens to Celina jogging up the carpeted stairs of her large cottage home on the fringes of Lier. It had been three weeks since Lenny and the boys had officially moved in. Just one week since he had applied for a job with the PTU.

'Sor-ry, Len-ny,' Celina purrs, 'I can't find that book anywhere in your bedroom.'

'Not in my drawer... under the bed, maybe?'

'No, I checked those places.'

'Shit. Can you rummage through the boxes under the stairs, please, Celina? It's... it's just, it's really important.'

He bends to pick up the sheet from the pavement, then squints at the photograph of Sofie again, listening with one ear as

Celina jogs back down the carpeted stairs. He turns the sheet over again and scans the notes... Such little information to go on. For such a big investigation. A young girl is missing. Yet one investigator, starting his first shift forty minutes ago, is the only person charged with finding her. With a mini-biography and one paragraph of information to go on. Lenny understands why the police can't investigate every missing child within the first twenty-four hours. It has to be that way. Even in cases where the PTU have legitimate concerns. Boys and girls go missing from every town, every day. For an hour, maybe two hours at a time. Three hours, maybe. Or six. Nine. An afternoon. An evening. Overnight. Police can't react to every single child who doesn't come home for dinner. In every single town. Ninety-eight per cent of those cases end innocently. Lenny knows that. He had built a business on it back in Dublin.

In Europe, a majority of missing person cases only become a lawful concern twenty-four hours after concern is raised. Only then do police forces label these cases as missing child cases, and no longer a case of a child's gone missing. The fundamental core concept of the People Trafficking Unit was to fill those crucial first twenty-four hours. But only for cases they legitimately felt may be people-trafficking cases. And people-trafficking moves quick. Really quick. It has to. No wonder Volgt told Lenny he shouldn't expect to be successful.

'I'm sor-ry, Len-ny,' Celina purrs down the line again. 'That book is not in any of those boxes.'

'Ah shit!' Lenny says, spinning to kick at the red-brick wall he had been leaning against. 'Where the fuck did I leave that book? I'm such an eejit. I packed so quickly... The move all happened so fast and—'

'Are you oh-kay, Len-ny? You sound so stressed.'

'Ahhh,' Lenny says, his eyes blinking. 'It's just... ah, It's just this crazy case they have me running. You won't believe it, Celina. I've to find a missing girl in twenty-four hours before it becomes a police matter, and they've given me one flimsy lead to chase. That some guy... a uh, what's-is name?' Lenny scans the notes again, 'a guy called Ruthgar Bilic *may* be a suspect. Just because he was released from prison two days ago and happens to live twenty-two-minutes' drive from where this Sofie girl went missing this morning.'

'Twenty-two-minutes?' Celina says.

'Yeah, that's what I'm thinking,' Lenny says. 'This lead sounds like a total guess, doesn't it? I mean, twenty-two minutes is what... thirty miles away? Don't we all live within thirty miles of somebody on the register?'

'I uh...' Celina hesitates. 'I don't know, Len-ny. I just know that if anyone can do this job, it is you. Just use your gut. Your gut always works out to be true, Len-ny.'

Lenny blinks his eyes. Rapidly. Soaking in the compliments Celina is always keen to offer. To anyone.

'Thanks,' he says. 'You're right. I was trusting my gut. That's why I was hoping you'd be able to read me a chapter out of that book. Where Betsy writes about contacting somebody through her Kindle. My gut is telling me that's how I solve this case. That's how I find out where this Sofie girl is. Not through this guy who lives thirty miles away.'

'Well, why don't you call her?' Celina says.

'Call who?' Lenny says.

'Betsy,' Celina says.

BETSY

I'm tired. Really, really tired. It's hard work carrying furniture up and down lots and lots of different steps. Too many steps. Too many steps for one house. Though carrying heavy furniture is not harder work than listening to my mom talking and talking and talking.

I've got more work done this morning since she took the ferry back to Holyhead than I did in all of the ten days she was here after I got the keys. At first I didn't mind her being here. Not really. I thought she could help. Help me around the house. But she didn't. Not really. She preferred to sit on the sofa, sipping tea, talking and talking. About him. Still about him. Always about him.

I squish the duvet up into a big ball and carry it across the squared landing, peeping over the top of it as I shuffle down the stairs. I love these stairs. I always will. Probably because I never knew what was up them. Not for years and years. They were like a mystery to me. And now I own them. I can't believe I actually own them. That I actually own everything in this house. I think Dod would be so happy that I own this house. He would be so proud.

I've turned his old bedroom into a library. It was the first thing I wanted to do when I got the keys. The library is the only room I got to work on while my mom was here. It's the biggest room in the house. Bigger than the living-room. Bigger than the kitchen. Much bigger than the basement. That's why it had to be my library. My library had to be the biggest room in the house. It took five days to clear the wardrobes out in between my mom talking and talking. Then three days to hang four long shelves on each of the four walls. I drilled the shelves in with an electrical drill I bought in a big, scary shop called B&Q, while my mom held the other end.... still talking. And talking.

I made too many shelves for the amount of books I have. Which was a surprise to me. Because I thought I had loads and loads of books. But I only filled three shelves. I'll fill the rest of them. All four shelves of all four walls in my library. I can buy as many books as I want.

Monica called the day after I got the keys to the house, to tell me *Betsy's Basement* had sold one point two million copies in its first three days. And that I'd already earned out my advance. I was shocked. And excited. And proud. Really, really proud. More proud than I was shocked or excited. The footage of me entering 166 South Circular Road for the first time in five years worked wonders. Or 'viral' as Monica keeps telling me.

I drop the duvet onto the brown floorboards in the hallway, then I stand in the doorway of the basement staring down the wooden steps before I slap a hand to my forehead, and I sigh. I don't know what I'm doing. There's just too much to do that I can't think straight. I need to sleep tonight. Sleep good. So I need to sort my bedroom out. Once and for all. That's what I need to concentrate on today. If I begin to get good nights' sleeps, then I will feel much better getting everything else in the house finished. Now that the library is done, I need to sort my bedroom.

'Bedroom, bedroom,' I say, spinning around to look at the

mess in the hallway. I repeat things to myself to make me concentrate on them sometimes. 'Duvet,' I say, pointing at the duvet I just carried down the stairs in a big ball.

Then I slap my hand to my forehead again and I glance up and down the hallway at what I need next. But I can't think... I can't think straight. There's too much to think about. Too much to do... Then, I jump back, my hand pressed against my heart, my slippers sliding on the floorboards. Scared. Frightened. The noise. A horrible noise. Like a duck squealing. Over and over again. Loudly. Really, really loudly.

I let go of my heart and I step towards the noise, towards the basement door, to where I push out a laugh... with relief.

I walk down the wooden steps and stare at it. Then I move really close to it. It's not moving. Not vibrating like my brothers' mobile phones vibrate when they ring. It's just staying still. Sitting on the carpet. Squealing at me like a loud duck.

I lift up the bit that comes off at the top, and the duck squealing stops... and there is quiet. The kind of quiet I really, really like...

'Hello,' I hear a voice.

I look down at the phone in my hand, then press it to my ear.

'Hello,' I say.

'Betsy! It's me. It's Lenny Moon.'

'Hello,' I say. Again. And then I don't say anything... I don't know what you're supposed to say on these old phones.

'Hey,' he says, filling my silence for me. 'Congratulations. I hear the book has been number one for three weeks now. You must be so proud.'

'I am,' I say. 'I am proud. Really proud.'

'Well, you should be... Well done you. Let me ask you this, have you settled in to 166 yet?'

I stare around the empty basement, then up the wooden steps where the mess of all sorts of stuff is lying on the floorboards in the hallway.

'Kinda. Not yet. Not really. I got the keys ten days ago, but I've really only worked on one room.'

'Well, it's a big old house, so it'll take time.'

I push out a laugh, then take the heavy phone from my ear and stare at it... not knowing what to say... when something that I could say comes to me and I press the phone back to my ear.

'How are Jared and Jacob?' I ask.

'Oh, how lovely of you to ask,' Lenny says. 'Well, Betsy, they're the happiest they've ever been.'

'In Belgium,' I say.

'Yep. Belgium,' he says. 'Only I'm not in Belgium. Not today. I'm in Prague. In the Czech Republic. On a job.'

'A job?' I say.

'I'm looking for a missing girl,' he says. 'She reminds me of you, y'know. I've been thinking of you every step I make in this case. And then... and then something about you came to me. It was actually from your words. Words you wrote in your book...' I sit down, resting my back against the basement wall, crossing one foot over the other, 'you wrote about contacting someone on your Kindle when you were in the basement, Betsy. You remember that?'

'Of course,' I say, staring over at the opposite corner of the basement; the corner I was sitting in when that exact thing happened.

'How did you do that? How did you manage to contact somebody through your Kindle?' he asks.

'I didn't do it, not really,' I say, shaking my head. 'Somebody else did it. A girl from the customer service team at Amazon asked me a question in the settings and the Kindle gave me an option to text back with her...'

'Customer service?' he says.

'Yes,' I say. And then I uncross my feet and sit up a bit more. 'Who is she, Lenny? Who is the girl who is missing?'

'She uh... she's a French girl. Her name is Sofie. She's seven years old. Went missing this morning.'

'I'm so sorry,' I say. And then I start to hope that whoever took Sofie makes her as happy as Dod made me. Only I don't say that. I never say things like that out loud.

'I'm gonna do my best to find her, Betsy,' Lenny says. 'And you will be the reason I find her. Because she has her Kindle with her. And I think your book has inspired me to try to contact her through her Kindle. So... it was customer services, huh?'

'Yes,' I say, nodding my head. 'The customer service girl just asked a question... that's all... and I answered. I answered by typing on the keyboard on the screen, trying to tell her who I was...'

'You're amazing, Betsy,' he says. 'I'm going to contact Amazon Customer Services now, see if I can get access to Sofie's Kindle.'

I look around the empty basement with the phone pressed to my ear, thinking of the girl. Sofie. Wondering if she's scared. If she's scared like I was when I was first taken.

'I hope you find her,' I say.

'I will,' he says. 'Thanks to you...' I think about what to say next. Maybe I should ask about Jared and Jacob again. Because he didn't really say much about them... and I really like Jared and Jacob... Only Lenny speaks before I do. 'I gotta go, Betsy,' he says. 'I really need to be quick... Thank you so much for your help. And listen... I'm so happy your book has been a big hit. It's the most amazing book I've ever read. You're a tremendous writer.'

'Oh,' I say, recrossing my feet. 'Thank you, Lenny. Please tell Jacob and Jared that the girl who bought their house thinks about them.'

There's a pause, and I wonder if I said something wrong. Something you're probably not supposed to say on these old phones.

'I will, Betsy,' Lenny says. 'You truly are an angel. I'll tell them. I'll make sure I tell them. And listen, I think about you. I do. All the time. I always will.'

'Let me know when you find Sofie,' I say.

'I will,' he says.

And then there's a horrible noise. Beeping in my ear. Lenny is gone. My first call on this old phone is over.

I put the top of the phone back down, ending the noise, and I stare around my empty basement again, feeling a little better. Better than I felt when I didn't know what to do earlier. Because I spoke to Lenny Moon. And I helped Lenny Moon. And he told me I was a tremendous writer.

I push myself back up to my feet and I walk up the wooden steps, to where I stare at the mess in the hallway again before kicking a big cardboard box out of my way before I grab at the top of the mattress.

'Right,' I say to myself. 'Let's get my bedroom sorted.'

I drag the mattress, sliding it across the brown floorboards, then lifting it a little over the lip of the doorway before pushing it all the way down the wooden steps. When it reaches the bottom, I suck in a breath, and then I follow, shuffling down the steps after it. I grab the top of the mattress, and then I drag it into the corner, the very back corner of the basement where my bed always was. To where my bed will always be. Then I kick it into place, to make sure it's straight, before I rub my two hands together.

'Perfect,' I say.

SOFIE

I listen for his footsteps. Sometimes I can hear him downstairs. Walking around. But he hasn't moved in so long. So, so long. Maybe it's not long. I don't know. I'm not good with knowing time. I don't even know how long I've been here. Tied to this bed rail. Ropes wrapped around my chest. And my elbows.

I have stopped crying, though. I cried again when he was tying me up and when he first left me alone in the bedroom at the back of the smelly house. But I haven't cried since. I don't want to cry. I just want to go. I want to walk through the fields all the way back to the orphanage. To eat all of the stale bread that will be left over from breakfast.

When I do get back to the orphanage, I don't want to leave it ever again. Not to go walking. I will only leave the orphanage if a family ever comes to adopt me. To take me to my new home. Until then, I'm going to stay in the orphanage. Every day. Even if nobody talks to me.

It's dark in this bedroom. But I can see the shape of my bag in the corner. He threw it there when he took it off me before getting the rope from under the bed.

I wanted to ask him so many questions. Ask him what he

wanted me for. What was he tying me up for? But I couldn't ask anything. Not through the black Sellotape. All I could say was 'hmmmm, hmmmmm.' I can just hear 'hmmmm. Hmmmmmm,' inside my own head. Every time I try to talk.

The Sellotape is not sore across my mouth. And I've got good at breathing through my nose. But I want him to take it off. To make me feel less scared. If he does take it off, I would promise him that I won't make any noise. That I will be quiet.

'Hello,' he says.

My head twists. And the bed creaks.

'Hmmm, hmmmm,' I say. Inside my own head.

'Yes, I am,' he says. 'I, uh... I've got the cargo I told you I could get...'

He's not talking to me. He's talking on the phone.

'What do you mean?' he says...

'Really?... How much would that—?'...

'Oh, wow,' he says... 'really?'...

'Okay... Okay, and you are sure about that amount?'...

'I'll call you back later....'

Then I hear footsteps again, the floorboards creaking... The stairs creaking, then the floorboards creaking again as he gets closer... and closer....

The bedroom door opens, and a bright light shines through it, and he stands in front of it like a shadow. A black shadow.

He doesn't say anything. Then he moves towards me... closer... and closer... until I can see his beard. And feel him right next to me. Breathing. He smells bad. So, so bad.

'I got to go out,' he says. 'Won't be long. If you make any noise while I am out, I will hurt you when I come back. Hurt you real bad.'

I don't want to cry. So I close my eyes to stop the tears coming out.

'Hmmm, hmmm,' I say, nodding my head.

He tuts. Then he pinches at my cheek. But even though I am really scared, I keep my eyes closed, so that the tears don't fall.

'Ouch!' I say. The soreness is right across my lips. Really sore. So, so sore.

'Shhhh,' he says, staring at me, the black Sellotape hanging from his fingers.

'I won't... I won't make any noise,' I say. Quietly. I don't sound like me. I sound like a baby. A baby trying not to cry.

'I'll be out for half an hour. If you make any noise while I am out, I will cut you.'

'Cut me?' I say, opening my eyes and staring at his hairy face.

His beard is all horrible and dirty. Some of it brown. Some of it red. Most of it grey. Lots and lots of different greys.

'You need some water?' he asks.

I nod my head. And when I do, a tear falls. One tear, rolling down my cheek.

He spins around and walks out of the shining light, and his footsteps get further away from me. Then a tap turns on. Turns off. And the footsteps come back. Closer... When his shadow comes through the light in the door, he is gripping a glass.

'For you,' he says, putting the glass in my hand. But my hands can't make it up to my mouth. Not the way he has tied my elbows to the bed rail. So he tuts again, takes the glass from me, and then holds it up to my lips and tilts it into my mouth. I take a big sip. But some of the water falls down my chin, then down onto my lap.

'Dekuji,' I whisper when I'm finished. I'm always polite. Even to a man with a ugly beard who has tied me to a ugly bed rail in a ugly bedroom. Maybe if I am nice to him, he will be nice to me. And won't hurt me. But he doesn't say anything after I said, 'dekuji'. He just drinks the rest of the water himself, before he picks up the black tape again and begins to rip more off.

'Please,' I say as he bites the Sellotape. 'I can't breathe. I can't...'

'Breathe through your little nose,' he says, stretching the tape out and bringing it towards my face.

'Okay, okay,' I say. 'Okay. I'll breathe through my nose. But, can you... can you turn the light on? Please. I'm scared. Scared in the dark. Please?'

'The dark doesn't hurt people,' he says.

'No. Please. I need... I need something. Give me my Kindle please. In my bag. The screen lights up. And I can read. I can read while I am here on my own. I won't make any sounds. I won't be able to. You can strap that Sellotape across my mouth, and I'll just lie here... reading. Reading my Kindle. And it will give me some light.

He looks at my bag, then back at me before sticking the black tape to my lips and then rubbing his hand all across it hard. So, so hard.

LENNY

12:50

Lenny turns into yet another street lined by white houses topped with rust-orange roof tiles, the phone stuck to his ear, a determination bubbling like it hasn't in years—not since the Betsy case.

'Absolutely, Mr Moon, we sincerely understand,' a classy British accent squeaks into his ear. 'And we empathise with and fully support Dr Volgt's cause. I watched him on a *TedTalk* one time, and he blew my mind open. I had no idea how many people go missing every day. We'll do whatever it takes to support the PTU's investigation... But I'll, of course, need to have you cleared by Dr Volgt.'

Lenny winces, sucking a cool breath in through the gaps of his teeth before he stops walking and squeezes his eyes closed in hope.

'I am a private investigator for the PTU. I just—'

'I know you are,' the British accent squeaks. 'I believe you.

But I require clearance for this. As a PI I'm sure you're well versed on clearance...'

'Of course,' Lenny relents sombrely. 'Can you hold the line for two minutes, Errol, is that cool?'

'Sure, PI Moon?' Errol says. 'For an enquiry of this importance... absolutely.'

'Thank you,' Lenny whispers.

Then he stabs a finger to his screen before tip-tapping against it.

As he walks on briskly, the bright white houses with rust-orange roof tiles he had been navigating fade in colour, to grey houses with even greyer roof tiles. He squints across the street to read the sign, then paces in that direction, the road ahead long and narrow, worn grey-concrete terraced homes lining each side.

As his fingers continue to tip-tap at his screen, he recalls how Sally often forbade him from owning a smart phone when he began his journey as a private investigator.

'They cost too much money,' she would complain.

It turned out to be an ironic projection, given that Lenny wouldn't have made any money as an investigator had he not had such a wealth of technology in his pocket. Or gripped in his hand as it mostly was.

He lifts the phone to his ear, as a tone throbs through it, then sucks a deep inhale and holds it deep in his lungs, filled with air and anticipation...

'Hello, Dr Chuck Volgt's office,' the soft voice says.

'Olette,' Lenny says, exhaling as he recalls her name, not just because she was kind enough to bring him a cold glass of ice water before his interview this morning, but because she reminded him of it when he rang this number just fifteen minutes prior, his back leaning against the brick wall atop Kobylisy Metro station. 'It's, uh... It's Lenny Moon. Again. I need to speak with Dr Volgt as a matter of urgency.'

'PI Moon,' Olette says. 'Investigators don't have minute-to-minute access to the chief. I'm not sure when it was that any newly-recruited PI needed Dr Volgt twice within the first hour of working for the PTU...'

'I'm sorry, I am. But, uh...' Lenny pauses, hesitates, his eyes blinking. 'I've figured out a lead that I feel has been overlooked in the case Dr Volgt has me working on. The Sofie Le Saux case. I just need one minute of his time. To sanction something on my behalf. One minute of his day could save a girl's life...'

Olette blows an exhale down the line, leaving Lenny wondering if she is impressed, or unimpressed, by his determination. Probably the latter, he feels, in the resulting silence, as she pauses... and pauses...

'Lenny, I like you. I do,' she says, her accent a pale Central European, her tone soft but determined. 'I've never seen anyone come in here and look as nervous as you did this morning. Look, because I like you, I'll get him on the line. But for one minute. And one minute only. I need you to know this doesn't happen. This is not how being a PI with the PTU works.'

'Olette, you are a dream. Thank you.'

Olette blows down the line again, before the orchestral music Lenny had heard repeat itself over and over atop the Kobylisy Metro station crackles through his phone. He cradles the sound to his chest, allowing it to provide the score as he squints at the sign drilled into the wall of one of the grey homes.

Ladza Street.

He turns on to the street, to notice it is no different to the other dozen streets he navigated to get her. It's dank, and grey. Unkempt. He counts up the houses as he strides by them. Sixteen... Eighteen... Twenty...

Twenty-two looks vacant; the windows almost as grey as the roof tiles, a curl of leaves miraculously growing from the concrete step at the front of its narrow hall door its wood peeling with faded paint.

Lenny inches his cheek toward the peeling paint, the orchestral hold music providing an ominous score... There's a silence behind the door. A dead silence. He leans away, then shuffles like a crab to the large grey widow and attempts to squint through it. But there's nothing to be seen, not through the grey curtains behind the grey window, building a grey wall between the inside and the outside... When, the orchestral score stops, suddenly, Lenny spins on the spot.

'What is it, Moon?' Volgt huffs.

'Sir, I uh... I have the chief officer of security at Amazon in London on hold. He said he will give me access to a Customer Service chatroom that will enable me to leave a message on Sofie Le Saux's Kindle... On one condition—that you give me clearance.'

'Another James Bond,' Volgt huffs. 'You won't last a month in the PTU, Moon. Like most of them.'

'Sir, you have to trust me. The Betsy Taylor case I worked on five years ago, she almost got found through her Kindle.'

'Yes,' Volgt says. 'That was six years in, Moon. We do not solve cases like James Bond within twenty-four hours. You, as a Level One PI, Moon, have one job to do: follow the lead you were given.'

'Sir, please...'

'Moon, listen to—'

'Sir, please. Just give me thirty more seconds of your time... Just hang there. Please.'

Lenny palms his phone, then stabs at its screen, before scrolling his finger across it, making the call a three-way call.

'Hello, PI Moon,' the British accent says.

'Thank you for answering so quick, Errol,' Lenny says. 'I have Dr Chuck Volgt on the line for you. To give me clearance.'

Lenny winces, pinching his shoulders together, his teeth

clenched. There's a silence... an awkward silence... Before a throat is cleared. Chuck Volgt's throat.

'Hello,' he grunts.

'Dr Volgt,' the British accent says. 'I am a huge fan of your work. What great work you and these investigators do at the PTU. I saw you, y'know... at a TedTalk. Not in person. On YouTube, but wow, you really blew my—'

'Excuse me,' Lenny says, interrupting. 'I was just hoping you might ask Dr Volgt to clear me for access to the, uh, Kindle. I am operating on a very tight time schedule.'

'Yes. Of course,' Errol says. 'Dr Volgt, this fine investigator here says he needs to gain customer service access to a Kindle belonging to a young girl, Sofie Le Saux, who he says went missing this morning.'

Dr Volgt clears his throat again. Purposefully loud.

'PI Moon..'

'Yes-ss,' Lenny says, squeezing his narrow shoulders even tighter.

'Make this call a two-way conversation between you and I, please. Then we'll get back to this man at Amazon, yes?'

'Sure,' Lenny says, nodding to his phone. He thumbs the screen again, then lifts it back to his ear.

'That Amazon guy gone?' Volgt snaps.

'Yes, Sir,' Lenny replies.

'Moon, listen to me. You were given a very simple case this morning. With a very simple lead. We couldn't have given you an easier start. You check out the address on your notes. That's it. What's the name of that guy, whose house you are supposed to be calling by?'

'Ruthgar. Ruthgar Bilic,' Lenny says.

'Yes, Bilic. Well, your job is to get to his home and—'

'I'm here. I'm here now. Outside Bilic's address.'

'You are?' Volgt says.

'Yeah.'

'Well, listen, Moon. You knock on that door, then investigate the man behind it... you hear me? That's what you were sent to do. To see if he knows anything about Sofie Le Saux.'

'Sir, yes, Sir,' Lenny says, nodding to nobody.

'Now, tell me...' Volgt huffs. 'What is it you think you can do with this Kindle clearance?'

'I can act as a Customer Service Representative. That's how Betsy Taylor almost got found. She was randomly asked about her service one day on her Kindle and was able to text the representative back. If I can get in, I'll be able to leave a note in Sofie's settings... If she turns her Kindle on and goes into her settings, I'll be able to exchange texts with her.'

There's a silence. Before Dr Volgt kisses his own lips down the line.

'Listen, Moon. You do the job you were sent to do. Investigate this Bilic guy. Knock on that door. If he's clean, which he may well be, you can go chasing any Kindle lead you want.'

'Oh, wow. Great, Sir. Thank you. I really appreciate it. Ehm... let me, just... ehm...'

Lenny fumbles with the phone again, then scrolls his thumb across the screen, bringing the British accent back to the conversation.

'Hello, chaps,' the accent says.

'Eh, Dr Volgt...' Lenny says. 'Can you uh... give me clearance for the Amazon Customer Service thingy...'

There's another silence... Before Volgt huffs.

'Please give clearance to PI Lenny Moon,' he says. 'He is an investigator working out of PTU.'

'Dr Volgt, you got it,' the British accent says. 'It is a pleasure to help the PTU in their investigation. PI Moon, I will drop that clearance onto the phone you are calling me from in about, let's say ten to fifteen minutes. It shouldn't take long. We'll be aiming to get to it to you as soon as we can.'

'So grateful to both of you,' Lenny says. 'I really am.'

Then a dead tone throbs, and Lenny looks down at his screen, noticing it wasn't Dr Volgt who had killed his line first like Lenny had assumed. It was the posh British chief of security at Amazon—off to clear Lenny access to Sofie Le Saux's Kindle.

'Moon!' Volgt shouts.

'Sir, yes, Sir,' Lenny says, pressing the phone against his ear, his teeth squeezed tight.

'Now do as I tell you. Knock on that door in front of you. Find out what Bilic has been up to since he got out of prison.'

Another dead tone throbs, and when Lenny looks down, his screen is blank again. Both lines dead. A rippling image of an older version of himself reflecting back.

He hides his refection in the deep pocket of his yellow jacket, then jabs the air, proud of himself. Proud that he had thought outside the box. That he may have even impressed Dr Volgt with his outside-the-box thinking. Though it didn't sound as if Volgt was that impressed. Maybe Volgt is never impressed...

Lenny glances back up at the narrow wooden door crying with peeling paint in front of him, then down at the curl of leaves growing miraculously out of the concrete step beneath it, before slowly stepping up beside them and, without hesitation, he rattles his knuckles against the peeling wood.

SOFIE

He walks over to my bag. Picks it up. Then unzips it and turns it upside down. Making everything fall out. My pencils. My copybook. My Kindle. My bottle of water.

'Kindle?' he says, picking it up and turning it round and round in his hands.

'Hmmmm, hmmm,' is all I can say, my head nodding, my fingers tip-tapping against my lap.

He walks over to me, then sits on the edge of the bed and stares his hairy face into my face... Really close.

'Just books, yes?' he says.

I nod my head. And another tear falls.

He reaches a thumb to my cheek... and wipes away the tear.

'If I give you this Kindle while I am out, you stay quiet... yes?'

I nod. Really big nods. Lots of really big nods. Making more tears come out.

He puts the Kindle on my lap and then turns around and walks his shadow out of the bedroom, closing the door tight behind him, leaving me in the dark, tied to this bed.

I reach for my Kindle and pick it up as much as I can. Then I hold down the power button until the light turns on.

I have fifty-five books on my Kindle that I have downloaded for free. I've read all fifty-five books lots of times. Lots and lots of times. And I have read the first pages of lots and lots of other books. As many pages as Kindle will allow me to read for free. I don't mind reading books over and over again lots and lots of times. Books are even better the more times you read them.

I flick through the book covers on my Kindle screen, thinking about which one I should read while I am tied to this bed... I stop flicking when I hear his footsteps again, going down the stairs, the floorboards creaking. And then... a door opens with a squeak. And slams shut... He's gone. Gone out. Leaving me alone in his smelly house. Tied to his smelly bed.

I press my finger at the cover of *Three Times Lucky* while I try to sniff the tears back up into my eyes and into my nose. Then I try to start reading. But it's not easy. It's not easy to read when your brain won't stop thinking and thinking. I didn't read one word for two weeks when I heard the family in Prague weren't going to adopt me. That they adopted a girl from Greece instead. I would lie on my bed in the orphanage just thinking... thinking about everything I could think about. About having a father and a mother. About having a sister. Two sisters maybe. One older than me who looked after me. And one younger who I could look after. I think I would be a great sister. Only nobody knows I could be a great sister. Nobody will ever know it. I think about what my real father and mother are like. Who they are. Where they are. If I have real brothers or sisters... somewhere. Anywhere. One time, back in the Paris orphanage, Marion Deschamps' mother came back for her when she was nearly two years old. Me and Anais-Marie used to say how lucky Marion was. Lots of babies from the orphanage got adopted. But nobody ever got to go back to their real parents. Except for Marion Deschamps.

I try to wipe my face. But I can't reach too much with these ropes tying my elbows to the bed. I can only reach to my chin.

Then I take one large breath in and out before looking down at the Kindle again... trying to force my eyes to read. But I can't get past the first sentence... Because of all of the thinking and thinking. And because of all of the thinking about what I am thinking about, another tear falls from my eye. I am so silly and so stupid. Why did I have to walk so far away from the orphanage? Why did I have to walk so far through the fields? It's all my fault. My fault that I ended up here... tied to a bed in a smelly house..

I try to stop thinking about thinking, so I force my eyes to read the first sentence. But a tear falls onto the screen before I have finished it. And now I am crying lots. But not loudly. Because I can't do anything loudly. I am only crying inside my own head. Inside my own ears. I wish I could lift my hand to my eyes. To wipe the tears away.

I try to sniff the tears back up into my eyes and nose, again... and then... a knock. A loud knock. At the door. Downstairs.

'Hmmmmmm, hmmmmmm!'

I try to shout. As loud as I can. But it's not very loud. I can only hear myself inside my own head. Inside my own ears.

'Hmmmmm, hmmmmm!' I try again. Louder this time.

I try to rattle in the bed. But it's not making much noise. Just a small creak. So, I sway and wiggle. And twist and turn as much as I can...

'Hmmmmm!' I shout it from the back of my throat this time. 'Hmmmmmmm!' as loud as I can. 'Hmmmmmmmm!' Rattling the bed.

Then, I stop... And listen...

Nothing. Silence.

Whoever is knocking at the door can't hear me. They have no chance of hearing me. I wonder if my shouting is even making it out of this bedroom.

'Hmmmmmm!' I try again. As loud as I can. 'Hmmmmmmmm!'

And then I sob. Lots of tears. So, so many tears. Falling down my cheeks. Onto the black Sellotape. Dripping off my chin. Onto the Kindle.

'Hmmmmmmm!' I shout.

I wiggle, and sway. As much as I can. Trying to rattle the bed. To make the bed make some noise. But nothing... nothing... except for the sound of my Kindle, falling from my lap, then skidding off the bed and slapping to the carpet.

LENNY

13:10

Lenny spins back around and with his two pointed shoes pressed together leaps from the concrete step like a penguin, his two hands hidden inside the deep pockets of his yellow puffer jacket.

There's nobody home. Doesn't look like anybody's been home since Ruthgar Bilic was sent to prison however many years ago. The sheet didn't even provide that much information. Neither did Dr Volgt this morning when he offered Lenny the job. He just said Bilic was involved in smuggling in some guise and was sent down for it. He got out two days ago. And happens to live twenty-two minutes away from where Sofie is believed to have been swiped. It's not much to go on. In fact it's nothing to go on, not if Bilic isn't home...

Lenny glances up and down the vacant, grey street, before sighing heavily and then relenting by pulling his phone back out of his pocket and thumbing the screen again.

He presses his thumbprint against the Facebook app, then proceeds to type the name 'Ruthgar Bilic' into the search bar.

Dozens of Ruthgar Bilic's show in the resulting list, though only three suggest that the profiles currently reside in Prague.

The first Ruthgar Bilic from Prague looks too young to be the man who lives in this grey house, on this grey street. He's only a late teen. Maybe early twenties. Acne scarring his cheeks. The second Ruthgar Bilic can't be ruled out. He's the right age. Somewhere in his mid-forties. A rough haircut and even rougher beard. Looks like he's been living a tough life. Certainly in contrast to the third profile Lenny clicks into. This Ruthgar Bilic is wearing expensive suits in each of his profile pictures. Is married to a woman who looks like she walked off the front of a magazine. And they share three beautiful sons according to the banner photograph across the top of his page.

'It must be this guy,' Lenny whispers to himself, clicking back into the bearded Bilic.

Lenny scrolls through the profile, noting a few shared memes is all his suspect has ever posted. There's nothing to go on. Except the profile picture. A face to the name. An ugly face. To an ugly name.

Lenny pockets the phone again, before swivelling and stepping back up on to the concrete step, his knuckles curled, ready to rattle against the wooden door... when behind him, there's a slam. And a cough. A really loud cough.

He glances over his shoulder, to see an elderly man limping away from one of the grey houses having pulled its front door closed.

Lenny leaps off the step with his feet pressed together like a penguin again, then looks up and down the street before striding across it.

'Excuse-y me,' he calls out in his awful European accent. 'Excuse-y me, Sir.'

The elderly man's limp turns to a shuffle, his pace quickening... But he doesn't get far before Lenny is standing in front of him, holding his hands out.

'Excuse-y me,' Lenny says, pointing across the street. 'Do you know anything about your neighbour, Ruthgar Bilic?'

'Nemluvim anglicky.'

'No. No, I uh...' Lenny says. 'I am asking about Ruth-gar Bil-ic. Number twenty-two.'

Lenny points over at the house with the peeling paint on its door. Then notices it is no different to any front door on the street.

The elderly man shakes his head, then offers a gruff.

'Nemluvim anglicky,' he says, grabbing at Lenny's shoulder, almost pushing him out of his way.

'I just... I just,' Lenny says as the elderly man shuffles by him. Lenny pauses, then sighs to himself, before his eyes round, causing him to dip his hand into his pocket, to retrieve his phone.

'Sir, sir,' he calls after the elderly man. 'Sir this man. Have you seen this man?'

He shoves the phone towards the neighbour's face, showing the Facebook profile picture of the bearded Ruthgar Bilic.

'Ahhh,' the elderly man says, nodding.

'You do know him... Have you seen him?'

'Vezeni.... Vezeni.'

'Vez-what?' Lenny says.

'Vezeni,' the elderly man repeats, holding his hands out, gripping air.

'Prison?' Lenny says.

'Eno,' the man says, nodding. 'Prison, Vezeni.'

'He's-a out. Out-a of prison. No more Vezeni..' Lenny says.

'Out?' the man says.

'Eno...,' Lenny says, nodding. 'He is-a out. No more Vezeni.'

The elderly man's lips curl downwards, and his chin rounds.

'Let me, eh...' Lenny says, thumbing his phone again. He stabs at the screen, then tip-taps against it, the elderly man rolling his heavy, yellowing eyes, itching to move on.

'No... wait, please,' Lenny says. He brings the phone closer to his mouth. 'This man was released from prison two days ago. Have you seen him?' he shouts, as clear as he can into the phone, before holding the phone out.

'Tento mum byl propuštěn z vezeni před dvěma duny. Video jsi ho?' a robotic voice says.

'Ne. Dlouho ne,' the man says.

'No. Not for a long time,' the robot translates.

'Damn it!' Lenny whispers to himself. He lifts the phone to his lips again. 'I have knocked on his door. But nobody is answering.'

He stretches the phone back out.

'Zaklepal jsem na jeho dveře. Ale nikdo neodpovídá.'

The elderly man huffs, then leans into the phone, whispering in his heaviest Czech.

Lenny squints, then brings the phone to his ear when the man has finished.

'Nobody answers their doors around here,' the robot says.

The man pushes at Lenny's shoulder again, and walks on, shuffling away from any further inquiries from the strange man in the funny yellow coat with the funny European accent.

Lenny looks up and down the long stretch of grey houses Ladza Street offers, stopping his gaze at number twenty-two again... wondering if Ruthgar Bilic is in fact behind it. Refusing to answer... Lenny forms his fist into a ball, then strides back across the street towards the wooden door crying with peeling paint... when a vibration inside his pocket stops him, his pointed shoes skidding to a halt.

He dips his hand into his pocket, takes out the phone and stares at the screen.

. . .

PI Moon. Please tap the red arrow to download the attached software to your phone. Once downloaded you will have access to the settings of Sofie Le Saux's Kindle device. Very best of luck. Errol.

SOFIE

I wish I could breathe through my mouth. Breathing through my nose makes me feel like I am not breathing right. And it is scary. Even scarier than being tied to the bed.

I suck in through my nose for really long and hold my breath as I try again. As loud as I can.

'Hmmmmmm! Hmmmmmm!'

When I stop, the breathing through my nose becomes fast again. In and out. In and out really fast. So, so fast. And I wonder if I should stop now. Stop trying to shout through this black tape. I can only hear myself anyway... inside my head. Inside my ears. Whoever was knocking on the door a few minutes ago is gone anyway. They must be. They haven't knocked a second time. They're gone. Gone for good...

My heart is beating the same as my nose is breathing. In and out. Really fast. So, I try to calm my breathing down, so that my heart might calm as well.

I feel tired. Really tired. As if I could go to sleep right here, right now in this bed. But I can't sleep. I need to stay awake in case somebody else knocks on that door. Maybe the next person might hear my screams. Maybe the next person will hear me and then break down the door and come and rescue me. Be my hero. Bring me back to the orphanage. To eat the breakfast leftovers.

I slip my foot off the bed and move it around the carpet as much as I can. To feel for the Kindle. But I can't stretch very far. I can't feel it... I am so stupid. So, so stupid. I try to stretch my toes as far as I can... but I can only feel the carpet. Why didn't I just hold on to the Kindle while I was rocking the bed? Why did I have to let it fall? Why did I walk so far through the fields this morning? I'm so silly. So, so silly and so, so stupid. Everybody knows I'm silly and stupid. That's why I have no friends. And no family.

My cheek leans on to my shoulder. And my eyes close. But then I move my head really quickly. Shaking it. Shaking it so that I stay awake. I don't want to sleep. Somebody might knock on that door again. And I'll be ready. I'll be ready to scream as loud as I can. Through the Sellotape. Through the bedroom door. Down the stairs. And out the front door.

I sit up as much as I can, to try to look down to the carpet. But I can't see much. Not in the dark. The ropes are hurting me. Hurting my chest. Hurting my arms. But I have to find my Kindle. It's the only way I will stay awake. I need the light of the Kindle. I need to read a book so that my cheek doesn't lean against my shoulder again and my eyes don't close...

I slouch down as much as I can again, and I bend my knee backwards and stretch my toes out as much as I can. Nothing... Only carpet.

'Tu es une fille tellement stupide, Sofie,' I say to myself. Inside my mouth. Inside my own head. I mean it. I am such a stupid girl. I should have held on to the Kindle. 'Tu es une fille tellement stupide!'

I feel more angry than I feel sad. Angry with myself. I make mistakes all the time. Why would anybody want to adopt a girl who does so many silly and stupid mistakes all the time?

My anger makes me kick. Stretching my toes back as far as I

can. Sticking my heel out. Kicking and kicking. Kicking around the carpet. It begins to hurt my arms because I am leaning so far down. But I keep kicking anyway. And kicking...

I can hear myself. Screaming inside my own ears.

'Hmmmmm! Hmmmmm!'

The bed rattles as I kick. And I kick again... when crunch! My foot lands right in top of the screen. I hear a crack. I definitely hear a crack.

'Non, non, non!' I shout.

I sweep the Kindle with my foot, then back-kick it closer to me. Scoot... Scoot... Until it makes a noise against the bottom of the bed. Then I try to reach my hands down as far as they will go. But they aren't going near the floor. Not with my elbows tied to the bed rail. My fingers can barely make it over the side of the bed. So, I try to slide the Kindle up the bed with my bent foot, my fingers stretching as far as they can go over the side of the bed.

'Hmmmmm, hmmmmm!'

The Kindle falls. And I breathe out. Sad. And angry. And tired. So, so tired.

But... I try again. I scoot the Kindle to the bed, then try sliding it up the side of the bed... Higher... And higher. Until my fingertips can touch the top of it. Not grab it. But touch it.

'Hmmmm, hmmmm,' I keep saying. Over and over again inside my own head. 'Hmmmmm, hmmmmm.'

I bend my knee more, to lift it higher. Higher again. It hurts. But I'm almost there... My fingers pinch at the top of the Kindle, and they can take it up further. And further. Over the side of the bed. Then next to my knee. Then onto my knee.

'Oui, oui, oui,' I say, resting the back of my head to the cold bed rail. 'Oui, oui, oui, Sofie.'

I grab the Kindle, then press my finger against the button below the screen, and as soon as the light blinks on, I can see a crack right down the centre. Just one crack. One straight crack down the very middle of the screen. But the Kindle still turns on. It's still working. I can still read from it. Through the crack.

I notice a grey bubble down the bottom of the screen. A warning in my settings. Flashing at me. Telling me the Kindle has been cracked. So I don't click into it. I don't want to click into it. I just want to read. I need to read. I need to read a book that will stop me from falling asleep.

When I touch the screen, I remember I was trying to read *Three Times Lucky* when the knock came at the door.

'Okay, Sofie,' I say inside my own head. 'Read...'

I whizz my eyes over the first sentence... first paragraph... then to the bottom of page one. I swipe the page away and begin whizzing my eyes over page two just as quickly. I probably don't need to read the words in this book. I know these words inside my brain. I must have read *Three Times Lucky* fifty times. Maybe a hundred.

I flick away page two... meeting Moses LoBeau for the first time on page three. I wish I was like Moses LoBeau. We are like each other in some ways. We're both orphans. Hoping to find a family. But she is happier than me. She has more confidence. She has more friends. She has people who help her. Maybe I've always just wished I was like Moses LoBeau. It's why I love *Three Times Lucky*.

I flick away page three... noticing the grey bubble underneath the page is still blinking at me. It's annoying when that happens. But I just ignore it. It will go away. It always does.

As I am reading page four I begin to think if I am even reading the words. Because I don't hear them inside my head. My eyes are looking at them. But I'm not saying them...

Instead, I hear a voice. Two voices. Outside. Passing by.

'Hmmmmm! Hmmmmm!'

I shout from the back of my throat as loud as I can.

'Hmmmmmm! Hmmmm!'

I stop. To listen. But I can only hear my sharp breathing. In and out through my nose. So I breathe in really slowly and hold it... to see if I can hear the voices again. But I can't hear anything. They were just passing by. They were just passing by...

But I try again. One more time. Just in case.

'Hmmmmmmmmmmm!' As loud as I can. Probably the loudest one I've done so far. But I know even before I've finished shouting that the noise is staying inside this bedroom. It's not loud enough.

I close my eyes. Really tight. And lean my head back to the bed rail again.

'Tu es une fille tellement stupide, Sofie,' I whisper inside my own head.

My cheek leans on to my shoulder again. And I let it stay there for a few seconds until I pop my eyes open and shake my head. Shake myself awake. Awake from the dark again.

I look down at the Kindle ... and stare at page four, thinking whether I've already read it or not. I can't remember. It doesn't matter. I begin at the top of the page anyway... even though that annoying grey bubble is blinking at me.

I tut again. And rather than read the words, I press my finger to the grey bubble instead. And the screen blinks, then a box pops up, covering the words on page four.

'A Kindle Customer Service Message', it says in a grey box. I tut inside my head, then press my finger to the grey box, and another box blinks open below it.

Sofie, my name is Private Investigator Lenny Moon. My job is to find you. And I will find you. With your help.

LENNY

13:20

Lenny grips his mobile phone tight in his left hand as he navigates the maze of grey suburban Prague streets, checking it every thirty or forty strides to make sure it hadn't vibrated without him feeling the tickle. There's a buoyancy in his step, even though he isn't rushing anywhere. He isn't even going anywhere. He doesn't even know where he is...

He thought about taking the metro back into the bustle of the Czech capital, close to the fifty-two-storey high-rise building he was interviewed in this morning. Being central feels like the most sensible place to position himself. Though he can't be certain. Not until that phone vibrates in his left hand with a message from Sofie, letting him know where she had been taken to... Instead, he has opted to keep walking and walking, a pep in his step because he had made a major breakthrough in such a tough case. Sending a help message to Sofie Le Saux's Kindle sure is better investigating than randomly rattling his knuckles against the door of a guy's house just because he had been released from prison. The Ruthgar Bilic lead is barely a lead at all, Lenny has convinced himself. The more he has strolled away from Ladza Street. It's barely investigating. It's guessing. It's stabbing in the dark.

As he turns into yet another street lined by grey houses with even greyer roof tiles, the sizzle he has been anticipating since he began walking in no direction whatsoever finally tickles his palm. And with an excited exhale, he turns the phone over and stares at the screen, his anticipation turning to quizzical quickly. It's not Sofie returning his Kindle message. It's an incoming phone call. From a number that's become familiar to him this morning.

'Hello,' he says, answering.

'PI Moon,' Olette says. 'I am sorry to ring you in the middle of an investigation. It's just... we have another case. A case the board feel you may be a better fit for.'

'Sorry?' Lenny says, his eyes squinting the length of the grey street.

'It's a young boy named Liam McLyn. He's from Ireland. Which is why Dr Vogt and the board feel you may be interested. He was holidaying in Prague with his family and went missing this morning. Police have not yet marked it as a missing person's case, but our board have declared it a possible trafficking case and have greenlit it to be investigated. It has a lot more information to go on than the Sofie Le Saux case. They feel you, being Irish, may be the ideal investigator for this one.'

'But I'm... I'm investigating the Sofie Le Saux case,' Lenny says, his brow dipping.

'We understand,' Olette replies. 'The board feel that Liam McLyn being Irish may entice you into—'

'No,' Lenny says, interrupting. 'I am right on top of the Sofie Le Saux case. I've made a breakthrough. I sent a message to her Kindle and I'm waiting to hear back from her...'

There's an obvious hesitation on the line. A silence. That eerily transitions to a deathly silence... Lenny shakes his head, confusion etched all over the features of his pale face.

'Liam McLyn is an nine-year-old boy who was—'

'I'm sorry, Olette,' Lenny says, interrupting again. 'But I'm in the midst of the Sofie Le Saux case.'

'I understand, PI Moon,' she says... Then there's another silence. Not as long as the first. But just as ominous. 'Not to worry.'

The line dies, leaving a dead thrill pulsing through Lenny's ear. He drops his hand and stares blankly at the screen, seeing his aged, confused face staring back at him again.

He had researched the PTU in detail when applying for the job as an investigator two weeks ago, excited about the possibility of becoming a cog within the unit that helped stem the tide of missing people through Europe more than any other organisation that has ever existed. Their website was mighty impressive. Glossy. Detailed. Professional. Yet since he had started working for them a little more than an hour and a half ago, they had proven to be anything but...

Here Lenny was, ninety minutes into an investigation, having just made a huge breakthrough in his debut case, yet the PTU were ringing to offer an alternative investigation. The Liam McLyn case.

'What the fuck is going on?' Lenny whispers as he continues walking, palming the phone into his left hand again.

'Don't expect to solve too many cases, Moon,' Dr Volgt had told him in his gruffly voice after offering Lenny the job this morning. At the time, Lenny felt it an odd thing to say. An hour and a half later, it seems beyond strange. *Don't expect to do your job?*

'Maybe it's just my role that's not meant to be successful,' Lenny mutters to himself. 'Maybe at my level, the chances of solving cases are near impossible... I'll get a promotion in time... to a level where I will be able to solve—'

His muttering stops. Then his walking stops. Because the phone in his left hand has tickled his palm again.

He turns his hand over and stares at the screen. A message. The message he's been pining for. From Sofie Le Saux's Kindle.

He sucks in a cool breath though his teeth before he exhales heavily just as he presses a finger to his screen.

I am so scared. Please find me. Please find me. I am so scared.

His breaths become gasps as he reads Sofie's innocent message over and over. Then he sways his jaw from side to side as he begins to repeatedly tip-tap his two thumbs against his screen.

Sofie. I will find you. I will. What I need you to do is tell me what you remember. Tell me what happened after you were taken. Where were you taken to? How far away were you taken? It's important you text me what you can recall from the time you were taken.

He pushes the arrow next to the message box, sending the text off with the sound of a swoosh. Then he grips the phone even tighter in his left hand and begins jumping up and down on the spot. Excited. Exhilarated. A rush of adrenaline sizzling through the veins pulsing at his temples.... Until he stops. Standing still. Feeling another self punch to the gut. He shouldn't be feeling excited. There's a seven-year-old girl missing. Missing and scared. Scared for her life.

'I'm gonna find you, Sofie,' Lenny whispers to his phone.

Then he sets off on his walk again. Walking to nowhere. Navigating the maze of streets lined by grey houses with even greyer roof tiles... waiting... waiting again... He throws his eyes to the pale sky, noting he is north of the city of Prague. West of the fields Sofie was walking in this morning when she was taken. He doubts a seven-year-old will even know her north from her south, or her east from her west. But Sofie reads. So she should be able to text him back; she should be able to gift him information. Information that will lead him to her.

He steps off, buoyancy in every stride, his mind whirring, before he is stopped in his tracks again. His phone sizzling in his hand.

He turns it over, expecting to see an update from Sofie. But it's not Sofie texting him. It's Celina. A text from home. His new home.

He taps at the message, then brings the screen closer to his face so he can squint at the photo she promised earlier that she would send. A photo of Jared and Jacob grinning their bucked teeth, their eyes squeezed shut with joy. Lenny pinches the screen, zooming in on his boys' faces, noting a stream of wet glistening away from Jared's eye. His son literally crying laughing.

Lenny presses the phone against his chest and inhales. Deeply. He did it all for them. Uprooted his life in Dublin to emigrate to Lier. And it's working. It's definitely working. This photo is proof of that. Twenty-one days of fresh Belgian air sure has brought the best out of his twins. Just like Celina promised it would... She sure is something...

The smile drops from Lenny's face when the phone vibrates against his chest, and he glances down, then presses his finger against the Amazon message notification.

A man took me and tied me to a bed in a house it is a grey house he said he had food for me but he had no food and he took me in his car. i can't remember that colour of the car but i could hear children when he was driving children at school. we took nine turns in the car i think it was nine turns I counted the turns

SOFIE

My breathing is really quick in and out of my nose. Not because I am scared this time. But because I am happy. So, so happy.

I don't feel all alone tied up in a bedroom inside a grey house anymore. I feel like I have somebody with me. Somebody to talk to. I never have anybody to talk to. Nobody has ever come for me. But private investigator Lenny Moon will. I know he will. He told me he will.

I grip the Kindle tight with both hands. And I stare though the crack I made in the screen when I kicked it, waiting on the grey bubble to blink again. I try to think how I can help private investigator Lenny Moon to find me... I wish I could remember the colour of the car. I don't know how I forgot the colour of the car. I think it was blue. But it was probably green. Or red. I don't know. And I shouldn't guess. I need to get things right. To help him find me.

I try to listen out while I wait on the grey bubble to blink. But I can't hear anything. Not over my breathing. But I want to listen. I don't need to be scared if the man with the beard comes back. I'll just pretend I'm reading a book on my Kindle.

When private investigator Lenny saves me and takes these

ropes off me, I'm going to give him the biggest hug ever. And tell him he's my hero. We could be friends. My first friend in Prague. My second friend ever. I wonder if private investigator Lenny Moon will be as good a friend as Anais-Marie was. Me and Anais-Marie used to spend every minute of every day with each other. Playing games. Or reading books. Or watching films. We used to talk so much. So, so much. About who our fathers and mothers are. If we had brothers or sisters. What it would like to be adopted. Were we too old to be adopted now? We used to ask that lots and lots of times. We promised that if any of us got adopted, then we would just come back to the orphanage every Saturday so we could still play with each other, still watch *Toy Story* together. Still read books together.

The grey bubble blinks and I feel a smile on my face as I press at it, even though I can't smile. Not with this black Sellotape on. But I know I am smiling inside.

Nine turns. Thank you Sofie. That is very helpful. You are doing great. Can you tell me how many minutes you were in that car for? Have you any idea how many minutes?

I suck in a really long breath through my nose. And hold it. Minutes... Minutes... How many minutes? I close my eyes and try to remember the drive. I heard children in a school. And I counted all the turns. I'm sure I did. If it is nine turns then it couldn't have been lots of minutes. Unless there was a long, long road we drove on that didn't have turns. But I don't remember a long, long road. Minutes... Minutes... How many minutes?

I remember Anais-Marie used to count time as chapters. Chapters in a book. She used to say that a chapter in a book was ten minutes. So when an adult at the orphanage would tell us there was ten minutes until soup was being served, Anais-Marie would say ten minutes was the same time as reading one more chapter. I think I was in the car longer than one chapter. I think it was probably one and half chapters. I think... I don't know. I'm no good with minutes. And I'm not good at maths. I remember Anais-Marie saying to me once that on Kindles, they tell you how many minutes it takes to read a chapter. I think of her every time I look at the minutes on my Kindle. She always wanted a Kindle. She always said that if she had a real father and mother and a real Christmas in the outside world, she would ask for a Kindle from Father Christmas. She said a Kindle would be the greatest present ever. But I didn't have my Kindle with me when I was in the back of the car. Counting my minutes for me. But I am sure I was in the car longer than it takes for me to read one chapter of a book. But not in the car as long as it takes me to read two chapters. I think one and half chapters is right. And if one chapter is ten minutes. Then two chapters is twenty minutes, and one and a half chapters has to be fifteen minutes. Fifteen minutes, I think I was in the car for around fifteen minutes.

I begin to type out my answer. Then I stop. And I press delete... delete...

I'm not good with time. And I'm not good with maths. But I need to get this right. Private Investigator Lenny Moon said I have to tell him what I know. Then he will be able to come find me. And save me.

'Reflechis, Sofie!' I say to myself. Inside my own head. 'Reflechis, Sofie!'

I close my eyes even tighter. And I imagine being in the back of the car again. Scared. My mouth taped shut. My breathing heavy because I can't breathe properly through my nose.

'Reflechis, Sofie!' I whisper inside my head again.

I close my eyes even tighter and think even harder. As hard as I can. The smells. The smell of petrol. The noises. The sound of schoolchildren playing. But smells and noises are not what Lenny is asking about. He is asking about minutes... minutes... How many minutes? If I can tell him how many minutes I was in the car, he'll know how far away I was taken. He'll know where to look. Then he'll know where to find me. I have to get this right. I need to get this right.

I open my eyes and start typing.

15 minutes

I think that's right. I was in the back of that car for the same time I would read one and a half chapters of a book...

I hold my thumb over the arrow, then I close my eyes again. Just to make sure. One and a half chapters. That is fifteen minutes. I think it's right. So, I open my eyes again, nod my head, then I tap my thumb to the arrow and send off my answer.

LENNY

13:40

Lenny swings his jaw from side to side as a splinter of thoughts race through the veins pulsing at his temples.

'About fifteen minutes from where she was taken,' he whispers to himself. 'Fifteen minutes... Passing a school along the way.'

He rests one shoulder against the grey wall of a grey house on yet another grey street, his fingers pinching at Google Maps, zooming inwards.

'Where the fuck are you?' he whispers again, before clenching a fist. 'Yess!'

He finds what he's looking for. San Pedro Orphanage. On the northern tip of the city of Prague, on the border of where the bright white houses with rust-orange roof-tiles transition to grey houses with even greyer roof tiles.

He pushes his finger so that he can locate the fields that web away from the orphanage Sofie would have been walking through this morning when she was swiped.

'Right,' he says, his brow sinking, his eyes squinting... his pupils darting 'She's about fifteen minutes from here... Where are the schools?'

He swirls his finger in a circle showcasing where Sofie could possibly be right now, if her reading of time is accurate. If she did only travel fifteen minutes in the car, then she's somewhere inside the radius Lenny's finger is circling; a large maze of homes that line possibly three, maybe even four hundred streets. And two schools. Lenny can tell by the education symbol on Google Maps. One school that is not very far from where he is standing now. About six turns away.

He exhales with a whistle... noticing that his finger is slightly trembling as it hovers over the digital map.

'Think, Lenny, for fuck sake,' he whispers to himself.

He swipes his way out of Google Maps, then logs back into the Amazon software and begins to tap his two thumbs to the screen, shaking his head as he types.

Are you sure you can't remember the colour of the car? Did you see a number on the door of the house you are being held in?

His head-shaking continues, even though he has already sent his text off with the sound of a cool swoosh. He's certain Sofie would have included the house number already. She seems a smart girl. She would have said that by now.

'Think, Lenny, for fuck sake,' he spits, again. Louder this time, the words flicking from his bottom lip.

His jaw begins to swing again as his mind races in splinters, like the maze of streets in the digital map. He's done so well so far. He knows that. He's made a major breakthrough in getting access to Sofie's Kindle. And now he has narrowed the search to a few hundred streets. Maybe two or three thousand possible houses. All of his own doing. He's not cussing at himself because he is disappointed. He's just... jammed... He's just stuck... Sometimes being almost there is a lot more frustrating than being nowhere near at all.

The phone buzzes in his hand, and he glances down to stare at Sofie's swift reply.

No I saw no number can't remember car colour

'Fuck!' he shouts, before looking up to see an elderly woman walking towards him, glaring at him.

Lenny sure hasn't endeared himself to many locals today. If any. They all seem to stare through him with disdain. As if they all know he took a free ride on their Metro this morning. Though that disdain seemed to happen before he rode that tram. Not even the three board members of the PTU were that enamoured by Lenny Moon. It was probably the yellow puffer jacket at first. Celina had reminded him more than once to make sure he took it off for the interview. But in his panic he had forgotten, swallowing up the beautiful navy suit she had handpicked for him last weekend. Dr Volgt pretty much told him he hadn't enamoured the board even when offering him the job. But Lenny's concern today shouldn't be how many shits the Prague locals give about him and his oversized yellow puffer jacket. His only concern is finding this girl. Saving Sofie Le Saux from being traded into a trafficking ring where she will be taken to who-knows-where. Volgt repeated to him over and over again this morning that swipers act quick. They have to act quick. They need to get their victims out of their hands as soon as possible. Sofie is likely to be moved on as early as tonight. Tomorrow morning at the latest...

'C'mon, Lenny,' he says to himself when the elderly lady has moved past him. 'Think, for fuck sake...'

He taps his thumbs against his screen as his mind is whirring, popping in and out of different apps even though he's not searching for anything in particular. He swipes into his text messages again, seeing the photo of his two boys grinning their bucked-teeth.

The sight of Jared and Jacob so joyous makes Lenny pause, his rapid thumbs hesitating. His racing veins no longer pulsing. He pinches at the screen, zooming into the twins' eyes, recalling how impossible it had been to get them to even smile back in Dublin, let alone cry with laughter.

'You did the right thing,' he whispers to himself.

It's not the first time Lenny's whispered that to himself recently. As if he is trying to convince himself that emigrating to Belgium was the right thing to do. He knows it was for Jared and Jacob's sake. There's no doubt about that. But he still needs convincing that it was the right move for him. He misses Dublin. Dearly. Misses the streets. Misses the people. Though he's not quite sure if he misses the people in Dublin as much as he missed Celina when she wasn't in his life. She understands Lenny more than anybody has ever understood him. She understands why he shouted and cussed at his twins on occasions. She had studied the effects Carter-Wiln syndrome has not just on those suffering with the disease, but those suffering from raising those with the disease. Lenny can open up to Celina in a way he's never opened up to anyone before. Not even Sally. Celina understands every guilt-ridden irritation Lenny has endured since his boys were diagnosed.

'You made the right move,' he whispers. Then he nods to himself. Almost convinced.

He swipes his joyous twins' faces away from his screen, then taps his way back into the Amazon Kindle Customer Service chat, his thumbs poised over the screen... trembling ever so slightly... He doesn't know what to type. He doesn't know how to extract the information from Sofie that will lead him to her.

'It has to be the little things. Little things she would have noticed. She wouldn't have noticed the door number... She would have been looking down the whole time. He would have had her head down.' Lenny kisses his own lips... 'So she wouldn't have noticed the number on the door... not if she was looking down...'

He sucks in an excited breath, then his thumbs begin to tip-tap... tip-tap...

Was there a step leading up to the front door?

He exhales softly as the text flies off with the sound of a cool swoosh before glancing up and down the grey street he had chosen to stop on. She could be in any house on this street. She could be in any of the many thousands of houses in the many hundreds of streets that web away from this one. But she's not far from here... somewhere within a thirty-mile radius. He's in the right area. Hanging around the northern suburbs has ended up being a better decision than restarting in the city centre. Another gut call that came right for Lenny. He sure would need to trust his gut in this new job. Finding children of trafficking within a day can only be a gut-led investigation. Certainly so when you're given one sheet of notes to go on. And twenty-four-hour cycles to work in.

He taps his thumbs to his screen again before holding the phone to his ear, just as a ringing tone trills.

'Hello.'

'Olette,' he says.

'Yes.'

'It's me... Lenny Moon.'

'Oh, Lenny,' she says. 'Are you calling to take on the Liam McLyn case? This one looks like a definite trafficking—'

'No. No. Listen, Olette. Forget the Liam McLyn case. I managed to make contact with Sofie Le Saux. She's being held hostage in a home in the northern territory of Prague. Not far from where she was taken.'

'Is this for real, PI Moon?'

'It is. Yes. I managed to text to her through her Kindle. I know she happens to be within a thirty-mile radius of where she was taken. Can we get more investigators on this—'

'Oh, PI Moon,' Olette says. 'I mean... all PIs are on an array of different cases. We don't exactly have a force. We can perhaps involve the, uh....'

In Olette's hesitation, a cool swoosh lands in Lenny's ear. And he drops the phone, to stare at the message.

Yes. There was a step a grey step. and it had weeds growing out of it

Lenny gasps, then just as Olette is about to speak, he talks over her.

'It's okay, Olette,' he says, excitedly. 'It's okay... I know where she is... I know where she is. I'm gonna go get her.'

He pushes at the red button on his phone, killing the call, then stares at Sofie's last message again. He can't be misreading it... A grey step with weeds growing out of it...

He punches the air, feeling the adrenaline flittering through him, then he pushes out a relieved laugh as he begins to tip-tap his thumbs against the screen.

. . .

I know where you are Sofie. I'm coming for you...

He stabs a thumb to the arrow, sending off his reply before tapping into the Google Maps app again and frantically typing.

22 Ladza Street

The app informs him the address is a seven-minute walk away from where he is standing right now. Back in the direction of which he came.

'Three minutes if I run,' Lenny says.

Then he races as quickly as he can, his pointed shoes slap-slapping against the pavement...

SOFIE

I lean the back of my head against the bed rail and smile. Even though I can't smile. Not with the black Sellotape across my lips. But inside I am smiling. Really wide. So, so wide. Because my hero is coming to save me. And I helped him to come save me. It is so nice to have a hero. To have a friend. A new best friend. Even if private investigator Lenny Moon is much older than me he still knows who I am. He will always be the one who saved me. We will be friends. We'll have to be. I'd write to him every day. Or call him every day. Or meet him every day. Whatever he would like a friend to do, that's what I would do.

I look up to the ceiling, then around the room. To see if I can see anything I haven't noticed before. But there isn't anything to see. It's just dark. Dark grey. Everywhere. I twist the Kindle around the room, to see if the light from the screen will help. But it doesn't. Not really. There's nothing in this smelly, dark room anyway. No clues at all. But I don't need any more clues. Private Investigator Lenny Moon is coming. Coming to save me. To be my hero. And my friend. Forever.

I twist the screen back to my face, then rub my finger against the crack I made when I kicked my foot against it. I kept calling myself stupid. *Stupid Sofie.* But I am not as stupid as I think I am sometimes. I helped. I helped a private investigator find me. Even though I was tied to a bed.

Anais-Marie is the only person who ever told me I wasn't stupid. She used to say, 'Tu es une saucisse intelligente, Sofie'. *You are an intelligent sausage, Sofie*. I think she meant I was intelligent. Not stupid. But maybe sausages are stupid. Maybe Anais-Marie was just being funny. She liked to be funny. All the time...

The grey bubble blinks down the bottom of the screen and I click into it, then press my finger against the box to read the new message.

Is the man who kidnapped you at home now?

'No,' I say, inside my head, before I begin to type back.

I think about what private investigator Lenny Moon is asking that for? I think about how long it will be before he is here...

I look for the F on the keyboard. Find it. Then continue typing. I am getting better at typing. Not faster. I am still slow. But better. I don't make too many mistakes anymore. I don't need to press the delete button all the time like I used to when I first started using keyboards to search for books on the Kindle.

No he is out he left me here are you close im scared

I read over my text before touching the red arrow, sending the message back to private investigator Lenny Moon, hoping that when he texts me back he is texting back to say he is just around the corner of this smelly house, just a few minutes away from saving me. From being my hero and my new friend.

I stare at where the grey bubble will blink. For ages... And ages... Waiting on it to blink. But it's not blinking... not yet... So, I try to read the book. Only I can't get past the first sentence. I just need to wait... to wait on private investigator Lenny Moon to break down the door. And come save me.

I rub my finger down the crack on the screen again. I am sad that I kicked it. But it will be all worth it. Because the Kindle saved me. I try to bring it to my mouth to kiss the screen, just like I did on the very first day I held this Kindle in my hands. But I can't bring it to my mouth. My hands can't reach that far. I kissed this Kindle for the first time in the front lawn of a woman who was having a clear out sale. I've only ever been at two clear-out sales. But they are good. Because people talk to you at clear-out sales. When I saw the clear-out sale in a garden on a street I was walking down, I went straight up the lawn and looked at the things for sale because I knew somebody would talk to me. She was a very pretty girl. She looked like the Paris girls you see taking boats along the Seine with fancy hats and fancy sunglasses. I think she walked over to me because I was holding the Kindle too long. I saw it for sale for €25 on the table. And wished and wished I had €25 to buy it. To buy it for Anais-Marie.

The woman asked if I wanted to take it. And I told her I wished I could. My best friend would love one of these more than anything. I told her all about Anais-Marie and how much we loved reading. And that Anais-Marie's dream Christmas present would be a Kindle if she had a real father and mother. I must have talked and talked for too long, because the woman put her hand on top of my hand and said, 'Prenez-le gratuitement.'

So I did. I took it. I took it for free like she said. I kissed the woman on the cheek, then I gripped and kissed the Kindle screen, just like I've done now, before I ran... and ran... all the way back to the orphanage. All the way back to give Anais-Marie the present she always wanted.

When I rest the Kindle back down to my lap, I see the grey bubble is blinking again. So I press my finger to it, then I click on the Customer Service box.

I have the man who took you in my sights. Just around the corner from where you are. He's going to lead me straight to you. I'm coming, Sofie. I won't be long.

LENNY

14:00

Lenny stretches the phone out in front of him as he races, studying the orange line that is leading him around the maze of grey streets towards the blue pulsing circle on his screen.

He realises as his pointed shoes are slapping against the pavement that he's not as fit as he should be. His stamina may be fine for that of a regular forty-three-year-old, but it's not near good enough for a forty-three-year old private investigator who may be required to sprint on occasion. Like this occasion. And he should start wearing trainers. For any investigation he takes from here on in. Pointed leather shoes won't do. Not around the concrete streets of European cities. He feels the thrill of the race and chase flow through him as he sprints, overriding the light burn in his chest.

'Proper fucking investigating!' he shouts, the phone still stretched out in front of him, his shoes still slapping against the pavement. He chicanes with a skid around the corner of yet another grey street lined with yet more grey houses...

Only two more turns of the yellow line to go.... A 'Z' shape of turns. Right and then left. Then he'll be at the blue pulsing circle. Then he'll be at 22 Ladza Street.

The burn in his chest catches flame. But the thrill of the chase wins out. There's no way he's stopping... not now. Not when there is only two quick turns to go.

He stabs two fingers to the centre of his rib cage as he continues racing, before skidding his pointed shoes as he navigates the right turn, following the zig-zag of the orange line... He sprints past a terrace of grey houses... then past a pharmacy... then a local shop...

'Holy fuck,' he says, his pointed shoes screeching and whistling to a sudden halt.

He circles his palm against the centre of his chest, his breathing heavy and panting, before he sucks in a deep exhale and takes three large steps backwards... So he can squint into the open door of the shop. Before tilting his head to the side...

'Is that... is that?'

He thumbs the map away from his screen, then pushes his thumb against his Facebook app. The profile pic he had been studying earlier is already on show. It was the last thing he searched for on Facebook. Ruthgar Bilic's bearded face.

Lenny stares at the screen, then squints up at the man inside the shop again...

Bilic sure has cleaned up a little, as if there were regular barber visits in prison. But that is definitely him queuing inside that shop. Unmistakably him.

Lenny pockets his phone, then walks into the shop himself, past the man with the beard queuing for the cashier, a bottle of water gripped tight in his hand.

Another self-punch lands in Lenny's gut as he saunters slowly down an aisle, his eyes wide, his breathing sharp and shallow. He presses the butt of his hand into his chest again and squirms his face in both discomfort and disbelief, his heart sinking. Ruthgar Bilic hasn't kidnapped Sofie. Why would he be out shopping if he has a seven-year-old girl tied up in his home?

Lenny holds the phone up to his face with both hands, allowing his thumbs to tip-tap against it as he continues walking the aisle.

Is the man who kidnapped you at home now?

'Shit,' Lenny whispers to the loaves of bread in front of him, before navigating the turn of the aisle, leading him back towards the front of the shop, where he notices Bilic is by now approaching the cash register.

'Definitely him,' Lenny whispers. He bows his head as he walks straight back out of the shop. 'Fuck. Fuck. Fuck. Fuck. Fuck! he spits through his teeth.

He leans the back of his head against the window of the pharmacy next to the local shop and is still cussing to himself, when his hand tickles... causing him to stare down at his phone.

No he went out are you close im scared.

Lenny gasps. And the adrenaline that had been deflating from him begins to pump again. Throbbing through him.

'Holy shit! It *is* him,' he says, leaning off the wall, to where he stands, zipping up his yellow jacket... and then tapping at his phone while he waits on Bilic to come out of the shop.

. . .

I have the man who took you in my sights. Just around the corner from where you are. He's going to lead me straight to you. I'm coming, Sofie. I won't be long.

Lenny looks up just as he presses at the arrow to send the message off, to see Bilic striding out of the shop, looking right at Lenny, then left to where he walks, squeezing the bottle of water tight in his hand.

Lenny follows, sheepishly, and then notices when they reach the next turn that the sign on the opposite side of the street is the exact same sign he had paused to read earlier this morning.

Ladza Street

He pauses to stare around the bend, waiting for Bilic to stretch into the distance, then he begins to follow, his hands deep in the pockets of his yellow puffer jacket, his walk now stiff and stern.

Bilic glances over his shoulder, startling Lenny and causing him to divert his stare, scratching at his temple. But when Bilic faces forward again and continues to walk on, Lenny quickens his pace... Until he is jogging... jogging straight towards Bilic who stares over his shoulder again at the yellow jacket rushing towards him, just as he reaches his own front door. The door with the step outside that has a curl of leaves miraculously growing from it.

'Nasleduges me?' Bilic shouts at Lenny.

Lenny stops a stride short of Ruthgar Bilic's bearded face and glares at him.

'English!'

'English?' Bilic asks, before squinting at Lenny's bald head.

'Are you Ruthgar Bilic?'

Bilic looks down at Lenny's pointed shoes, then all the way back up the length of the oversized yellow puffer jacket.

'What if I say, 'no'?' Bilic replies.

Lenny removes a hand from his pocket, his phone nestled inside his palm, before flicking his wrist to show Bilic his own Facebook profile picture.

'You sure fucking look like him. And you also happen to be standing outside his house. Open the door.'

'Are you police?'

'Open the fucking door, Bilic.'

Bilic pushes a laugh through his nose, then spins on his heels, tossing his bottle of water to the concrete, and striding away, his arms swinging as hard as they can, propelling him forward.

But Lenny sticks out a leg, catching Bilic's back foot at the top of its stride, tripping him to the pavement. His hands slap against the concrete, and before he can rise again Lenny is on top of him, gripping his arm into a hold behind his back, and dragging him with a choke hold of the neck to his feet—a technique he had learned on day one of field duty as a trainee Garda back when he and Sally were happy. He grips Bilic's wrist behind his back even tighter, then breathes heavily into his ear from behind.

'I said, open your fucking door.'

He drags Bilic towards the front door of number twenty-two, causing him to groan in pain before sucking an air gulp down his throat, his mouth drooling as he pants.

'Take your keys out of your pockets and open the fucking door!' Lenny snarls.

Bilic swivels and twists, but Lenny's grip is too tight, too controlling. There's no way out for Bilic, not unless he is willing to dislocate his own elbow and tear his wrist bones to shards.

So, he tentatively reaches his free hand into the pocket of his jeans, and then, sucking down another gulp, drool still hanging from his bottom lip, he slides the key slowly into the lock... and turns it...

SOFIE

When the key turns in the door, I hear a slap. A slam. As if the door opened hard. And fast. And I feel scared at first... But when the floorboards creak I feel excited. So, so excited. Because I hear two voices. I can't hear what they're saying. It sounds like mumbles. But it is two voices. Two men. The man with the beard who took me. And private investigator Lenny Moon. Who is here to save me. I breathe in and out quickly though my nose and my lips are trying to smile behind the Sellotape. I can't wait until these ropes are taken off me. And I can hug my hero. My new friend.

There's another slam noise downstairs. And then voices. Louder. Speaking English. Definitely speaking English. I hold in a big breath, so I can listen more clearly, without the noise of my breathing, but the voices are back to mumbles.

I look down at my lap and pick up my Kindle again, kissing the screen just like I kissed it on the day I was given it for free at some pretty Paris girl's clear-out sale. The Kindle saved me. I saved myself. And private investigator Lenny Moon saved me. Three heroes. All in one.

I remember gripping the Kindle this tight as I ran all the way back to the Pairs orphanage on the day I got it from the clear-out sale. I like to walk. But I don't really like to run. But that day I ran, and I ran, and I ran. As fast as I could. When I got through the doors of the orphanage I ran into the back yard at first. Because Anais-Marie liked to hang from the old swing bars when she wasn't reading a book or watching a film with me. But she wasn't there. So, I raced back inside and up the large stairs, before turning at the top and running up the small stairs to the very, very top where all the children's bedrooms were. I was so excited. So, so excited. As excited as I am feeling right now. Because Anais-Marie was getting the one thing she wished for from a father and a mother. A Kindle.

By the time I reached the tops of the stairs I was so tired, and I couldn't run anymore. So I just walked fast, all the way down the corridor, until I got to her door.

'Anais-Marie,' I shouted. I knocked. 'Anais-Marie.' I knocked again. Hard. But she wasn't answering. And she wasn't out the back yard. Hanging from the old swing bars like she usually was. 'Anais-Marie!' I shouted, as I walked back down the corridor... before turning down the narrow steps. Which is where I saw Paulina. One of the adults. Paulina turned her lips down and touched my shoulder.

'Oh, Sofie,' she said. 'Anais-Marie a été adoptee.'

I fell to my knees. It was at the bottom of the narrow stairs. On the landing. And I cried. And cried. For lots of reasons. Because my best friend was gone. Forever. To live with her new family... Somewhere. Anywhere... And because I was the oldest in the orphanage now. The only one this age who hadn't been adopted. I tried to be happy for Anais-Marie. But I couldn't be. Not really. I was too sad. So, so sad.

The voices start talking again, and then I hear the creak at the bottom of the stairs... And then the creaks come up the stairs. Two men. Talking. And walking. The talking getting louder. The walking getting louder. The floorboards creak and more... and more... as they get closer to me. And the bedroom door pushes open, and the bright light shines in. The two of them walk inside. Private investigator Lenny Moon. And the man with the beard.

Private investigator Lenny Moon's shadow walks towards me. And my eyes go really round, staring at him. Because he is small. So, so small for a hero.

LENNY

14:15

A waft sucks its way to the back of Lenny's throat as soon as he steps foot inside the house and, with disgust, he blows a heavy exhale through Bilic's hair, gripping his arm even tighter behind his back.

'The fucking stench in here,' Lenny snarls.

The scent he is disgusted by is warm. And dry. With heavy notes of cannabis. Definitely cannabis. And mould. And damp. Like dirty socks left out in the rain. The home appears at first glance to be as grey inside as it is outside; the discoloured curtains heavy across the window acting like a dam for the daylight.

'Would you not open a window?' Lenny snarls into Bilic's ear.

'I'm not used to windows,' Bilic responds. 'I haven't seen a window in eight years.'

Lenny grips even tighter before... twisting at Bilic's wrist. 'Oi, oi, oi,' Bilic pushes out in pain. 'Are you police?'

'Kinda,' Lenny says, his eyes darting over Bilic's shoulder and around the grey room.

'What does 'kinda' mean?' Bilic asks, sucking up strings of his saliva.

Lenny pushes a laugh into Bilic's ear, then he drives him towards the door at the back of the cramped, damp room, which he kicks open to find a kitchen as grey as the street, dank black curtains pulled across the back window.

He spins Bilic around, leading him back out through the living room towards the bottom of the narrow stairs.

'What do you mean 'kinda'?' Bilic spits out as he is being pushed up the first step, his breathing short and sharp, his neck gripped tight by Lenny's wiry bicep.

When they reach the top, Lenny leans them both towards the small bathroom and he peers inside. Even the bathroom is grey. Though it is providing the only daylight inside the house through a frosted window. He spins Bilic back around to face the squared landing, where he notices the back bedroom door is the only door closed. So, he pushes Bilic towards it, then reaches across his shoulder to push it open with a silent purr.

The bedroom is dank and grey, with flickers of dust providing a glowing shower. Lenny squints at a crack in the thick grey blinds pulled across the window before pushing Bilic away and stepping towards the bed, its grey duvet creased and wrinkled.

'Where the fuck is she?' Lenny says, staring back over his shoulder.

Bilic's eyes squint.

'She?'

'Where's the girl you took from the fields this morning? Where the fuck is she?'

Bilic laughs. A cackled laugh that riles Lenny into stomping towards him, pinning him against the wall of the bedroom and gripping a hand around his neck.

'Where the fuck is she?'

Bilic squirms, shaking his head from side to side, coughing... then choking... spluttering...

Lenny unwraps his fingers and pushes his forearm to Bilic's chest instead, pinning him to the wall.

'She?' Bilic says, coughing again. 'I thought you were here to take my weed.'

Lenny leans away, taking his weight off Bilic and stepping a long stride backwards, his eyes blinking rapidly, his fingers scratching erratically at the stubble above his ear.

'Sofie! Sofie!' he shouts.

But the only response he hears is the cackled laughter of the bearded man standing across from him.

'Holy fuckin' shit!' Lenny whispers to himself. 'Holy fucking shit. She's not here.'

Bilic's laugh drives Lenny out of the bedroom. Into the squared landing to where he spins in a circle, mirroring the swirling of his mind. He washes a hand over his bald head as he begins to shuffle down the narrow stairs, just as Bilic creaks onto the landing above him... still laughing.

'I'm only out of prison two days and you think I'm swiping girls? Get out of my house, you mother fucker.'

He laughs again, driving Lenny through the dank, dirty living room, to where he snatches at the front door and stares down at the leaves miraculously growing out of the concrete step. The self punch to the gut that is usually so familiar feels heavier this time. Much heavier. And there's no respite from it. The impact continuous. He shuffles his pointed shoes, while gripping his stomach, down the pavement to the house next door... to number twenty. To where he notices another leaf curling up from the concrete step... Then he shuffles across the street to number seventeen. To see more leaves. And moss. And grass. Growing not just from the concrete steps. But the kerbsides. Leaves growing through concrete sure isn't that miraculous. Not around here.

He hears Bilic's laugh again. Not repeating in his head. But from the doorstep of number twenty-two over his shoulder. Still goading him. Still driving him away. Past the sign for Ladza Street that Lenny had stopped to read twice this morning. Then around the first corner, to where he rests against the wall of another grey house to catch up with his breathing. To catch up with his reality. To swallow. To gulp. And then to bend over. Resting his hands to his knees.

'Holy fucking shit,' he whispers. Again.

When he stands back upright, he covers his face with both hands and tries to think... think it through. The portrait of Sofie most prominent in his mind. He told her he was coming... that he was coming to save her... He still can... He still has a thirty-mile radius to go on. He still has contact with her. With Sofie. Through her Kindle. He still has time.

He snatches his phone from the pocket of his yellow puffer jacket and punches his way into the Amazon Customer Service messages, then hovers his two thumbs over the screen... poised...

He doesn't know what to text. He doesn't know how to let her down... How to admit to her that he got it wrong. That he isn't around the corner...

Suddenly, the screen blinks brighter and a message appears. Straight into the Kindle Customer Service Box.

Lenny Moon. This is not Sofie.

Lenny widens his eyes as he rereads the message. Over and over again. A half-dozen times. Until another message blinks below it.

I have the Kindle now.

. . .

Lenny blows out a whistle, his jaw tightening, tensing, then slowly beginning to swing from side to side...when the screen gets brighter... another message.

I can type quicker. And I can answer some of the questions you've asked better.

Lenny blinks his eyes, then he begins to text back, his thumbs tapping rapidly... He shakes his head, then deletes what he had typed out, before wiping a hand across his bald head, then down his stubbled face, to where his fingers grip his chin... when another message blinks onto the screen.

I am tied up too. On the bed beside Sofie.

'What the fuck?' Lenny says, his eyes widening. Then he thumbs at his screen again, and without deleting it this time, he presses at the red arrow, sending his question off to the cool sound of a swish..

Who the hell is this?

He begins to pant heavy, before spinning the heels of his pointed shoes around in a circle, squinting at row after row of grey terraced houses. Then the phone lights up again in his hand and he glances down at it.

My name is Liam McLyn.

To be continued…

WHATEVER HAPPENED TO LIAM MCLYN?

Check out the opening chapter on the next page...

LIAM

I look at him. And he looks at me. And he smiles. And then he stares straight ahead again. To look at the road. So, I look out the passenger side window, and I start to think he might not be going the right way.

'It's. The. Grand. Hotel,' I say. And when I say it I know I sound funny, because I change my voice when I am talking to someone from a different country. I speak slower. And more careful. So that they understand me. I spoke that way with the football coach who was teaching us this morning.

'Yes,' the man says. 'This is the right way.'

It seems I am longer in his car than I would have been walking. But I was happy for the lift. Because I had been playing football for a long, long time and my feet needed a rest. And I wanted to get back to the hotel as quickly as possible. Because me and Mammy and Daddy and Susan are going to the Prague Zoo today.

I was looking around the corner to make sure it was the right way to turn when this man pulled over in his blue car. And asked if I was lost.

'Is The Grand Hotel this turn?' I asked him. Even though I

knew it was. He smiled at me. And he looked nice and helpful when he smiled. Even though his face was covered by a bushy beard.

'It's uh,' he said. Then he leaned over and opened his passenger door. 'Let me drive you back to The Grand Hotel. It's not far.'

My dad never lets me sit in the front passenger seat of his car back home. So I was excited. And got into the blue car. But now I think I shouldn't have got in. The man is driving me the wrong way. This is definitely the wrong way.

'Are you sure?' I ask. 'I thought the hotel was closer than this...'

'I'm just showing you a bit more of this beautiful city,' the man says. 'Don't worry, boy.'

I try not to worry. Even when the white houses we were driving around turn to grey houses and it looks like we are getting further away from where the hotel is.

'It's just...' I say, looking up at him again. 'My mammy and daddy are taking me and my sister to Prague Zoo this morning. They said we could go when I got back to the hotel after I did my football practice. They didn't want me to do the football practice this morning. But I begged and begged. And I promised I'd get back to the hotel as early as I could.'

He looks at me and smiles behind his beard again. He looks friendly. Really friendly. But I wish I had have just walked back to the hotel. And not gone on a drive looking around the city.

'We won't be long,' he says. 'Two more minutes.'

He keeps driving. Turning on to more streets that are all grey and not bright white which is what the hotel is. The hotel is really bright white. As if it was painted white yesterday. And probably the day before that. That's what my dad said on the first day of our holiday.

'They must paint Prague every day.'

I wasn't sure if he was joking. Because the buildings do look like they've been painted every day. But my mammy laughed, and then I knew my daddy was only joking.

'Where are you from, boy?' the man asks.

'Ireland,' I say. 'I'm from County Cork, ever heard of it?'

'Yes, of course,' he says. 'Roy Keane.'

'Yeah,' I say. 'Roy Keane and Denis Irwin. I'm from the same town as Denis Irwin. Near Turners Cross. Do you know who Denis Irwin is?'

'Of course,' he says.

'Are you a Manchester United fan?' I ask.

'I am a Benfica fan,' he says.

'Benfica?' I say. 'Portugal?'

'Yes,' he says.

'Why do you support them?' I ask.

'I am from Portugal,' he says. 'When I was a young boy like you, I lived just outside Benfica.'

'Ohhh,' I say.

'You support Manchester United, yes?' he says.

I look down at the crest on my jersey.

'Course,' I say.

'Tell me, what is your age, boy?' he asks.

'Nine,' I tell him. 'I'll be ten in November.'

'Oh,' he says.

Then he pulls the car over to the side of the road and when he turns the key and the engine goes off, I stare up at him at first. Then back out the passenger side window.

'I need to get to the hotel. My mammy and daddy..' I say. And when I say it I think I might cry. Just a little bit. So I stop talking...

'I won't keep you long,' he says. 'I just need to get something from my house. For you. A football that I think you would like. It was signed by Eusebio.'

'Eusebio?'

'Yeah.... Eusebio. One of the greatest footballers of all time,' he says.

I shrug my shoulder.

'Not better than Ronaldo,' I say.

'No, course not,' he says. 'Only Lionel Messi is better than Ronaldo.'

He turns around, opens his car door and steps out. And he pauses, looking up and down the street before walking around the car, to the passenger side door.

'Ronaldo is better than Messi,' I say as soon as he opens it.

'Shhhh,' he whispers, putting his finger to his lips. 'You need to be very quiet around here okay?'

'Okay,' I say. 'But uh... can we go back to the hotel after you give me the football?'

He smiles. And nods.

'Yes,' he says.

He pulls the door open wider and I get out of the car to get the football. The football signed by... by...

'What's the name of the footballer who signed—'

'Shhhhh,' he says. Like the way my teacher shouts 'shhhh', at me at school. And I feel bad. Bad because he asked me to be quiet and I couldn't stop asking questions. My daddy says that to me all the time. That I don't stop asking questions.

'Jesus, Liam,' he says lots and lots. 'You'll make a fine journalist one day.'

I think I might be one when I grow up. A journalist. If I don't make it as a professional footballer. I might set up my own Fan channel on YouTube. Or I'd be a fireman. Being a fireman seems like a cool job. But a professional footballer first. If that doesn't work out, I'll set up a YouTube channel called Liam's Analysis. And if that doesn't work out, I'll be a fireman. A really brave fireman.

He walks to a door that used to be blue but is faded now with a faded number seventy-eight on it and steps up on to a concrete step to open it. When I look inside I see that his house is small. Really small. He has two chairs like ones we have at the small kitchen table. And a tiny TV on the ground. Much smaller than the TV I have in my bedroom.

He looks poor. Poorer than he looked when he smiled at me. When he smiled at me, I thought he looked happy. But his house looks sad.

'Come in,' he says, opening the door wider. 'The football is upstairs.'

I stare straight up the stairs. They're really small and skinny. Like the stairs to our attic.

'I think I would like to go to the hotel... please,' I say. And I step towards the door. But he closes it. And I think I feel scared. I can feel it, in my belly.

'No, please,' he says. 'Let's get that football. Signed by Eusebio.... After you.' He points up the stairs. 'And then... I'll drive you straight back to the hotel. Hey, how old is your father?' he asks.

'Thirty-four. No thirty-six. My mam's thirty-four,' I say.

'Your father will know who Eusebio is. You could give the football to your father as a gift. He'd love that.'

I look up the tiny stairs. Then back at him. And he doesn't look so friendly. Not anymore. He's not smiling. And his face has changed.

'I'll follow you,' I say. I am scared. I know I am. But I'd be more scared if he was following me up the stairs. So I tell him that he has to go first.

He walks up the first wooden step and it creaks. Loud. But the second one he steps on doesn't creak. And then I follow him. On to the creaky first step. And I think I remember my grandad talking about Eusebio... one time. A long time ago. When grandad was alive.

'Is this your house?' I ask.

'It is,' he says.

And when he reaches the landing at the top, he turns around and whispers to me.

'Boy, you sure do ask a lot of questions... C'mon.'

He walks to the door at the back of his small house. And opens it wide to let me walk through.

As soon as I walk inside my belly tells me I'm scared. Really scared. Because all I can see is a small light. On the bed. And when I step closer to the light, I see it is lighting up a face. A girl's face. Her eyes are really round. And really wide. And she's mumbling. Mumbling because there's black tape across her mouth.

'I'm so sorry,' he says from behind me. 'But I have no choice...'

Then I feel Sellotape across my mouth...

FROM INTERNATIONAL BESTSELLING AUTHOR

DAVID B. LYONS

WHATEVER HAPPENED TO LIAM MCLYN?

BOOK FOUR OF THE LENNY MOON NOVELLA SERIES

WHATEVER HAPPENED TO LIAM MCLYN

is available by using the link below.

https://pge.me/LiamMcLyn

The end.

ACKNOWLEDGMENTS

This entire series is dedicated to my devoted readers.

Thank you so much for investing your time and money on my stories.

If you have a spare minute, please leave a review on Amazon for any of the novellas you have read. It would mean a lot.

A big thank you goes to Nastasia and the team at Stardust Books for the wonderful artwork they produce for the covers of these novellas. As well as to my editorial team of Maureen Vincent-Northam, Brigit Taylor, and Deborah Longman.

Made in the USA
Middletown, DE
31 May 2024

55100918R00073